MURDER IN MARRAKECH

Alan Ross, on a hitch-hiking tour of North Africa, watched George Dawson die in the central square at Marrakech. It looked like an accident, but someone resented Alan's interest in the dead man's niece. A falling wall, a gleaming knife, and the chain of accidents began to mount up to murder. Somewhere the mystery linked with the past. Alan Ross and Cathy Dawson followed the slender threads until there was no choice but to rendezvous with death under the scorching desert sun.

CHARLES LEADER

MURDER IN MARRAKECH

Complete and Unabridged

LINFORD
Leicester

First published in Great Britain

First Linford Edition
published 1998

British Library CIP Data

Leader, Charles, *1938 –*
    Murder in Marrakech.—Large print ed.—
Linford mystery library
    1. Detective and mystery stories
    2. Large type books
    I. Title
    823.9'14 [F]

ISBN 0–7089–5289–5

Published by
F. A. Thorpe (Publishing) Ltd.
Anstey, Leicestershire
Set by Words & Graphics Ltd.
Anstey, Leicestershire
Printed and bound in Great Britain by
T. J. International Ltd., Padstow, Cornwall

This book is printed on acid-free paper

Prologue in Cairo

The old man glared under the threat of the gun, his knotted hands gripping at the edges of his chair until the knuckles gleamed as though the white bones were about to burst through the tightened skin. The gun, an ugly black automatic, was held loosely, confidently. The old man stared past it into a smiling face with perfect teeth and sardonic eyes. A few feet away a third man stood grim and silent, his wrists manacled in front of him. He was the old man's son.

It was shortly after sunset and the air was still sticky with heat here in the small room at the back of the café. The door was closed but there was one narrow arched window that was open to admit the sounds and smells of the Cairo street. There was silence but for the distant, unrelated sounds from the window and the droning buzz of a fly that haunted the shadowy corners of the room.

1

The old man glanced for a moment at his son's face, but the expression there was tightly controlled and unreadable.

Outside the door an old Egyptian woman shrank away from the amused glances of the two men who waited by the bar of the empty café. Sometimes she glanced at their faces and sometimes at the smooth leather holsters that each man wore on his right hip, the flaps were unbuttoned and she could see and was almost hypnotised by the black butts of the revolvers. But mostly she stared at the door where her husband had received the Egyptian officer who had brought the son she had not seen for many years. She had seen the shiny glitter of steel on her son's wrists and wondered what it was that he had done wrong? She wondered too how her husband could help? She was badly worried.

The old man's left foot shifted harshly across the threadbare carpet. There was no right foot, and no right leg. The old man's wooden crutch leaned against the far wall, and he had needed it for almost forty years. His face had the expression of a bear at bay, and his eyes glowered dangerously despite his handicap and his age.

"Well," he demanded bitterly. "Is it a bargain?"

The Egyptian officer smiled.

"This — " he tapped the breast pocket of his jacket with reverent care, " — may, or may not have the value that *you* place upon it. True your story sounds wholly plausible and I shall obviously investigate more closely. But I cannot release your traitorous son in return. Even if I wished to do so it is not in my power."

The old man's mouth contorted with the tightening of his jaw but his words came out clearly as he asked,

"Then why did you bring him?"

"Because you would not have talked otherwise. Your offer interested me. It was worth pursuing. If these notes you have just given me prove their worth then perhaps some small financial reimbursement can be arranged."

"You gave your word. My son — "

"Your son is a traitor. I do not feel obliged to keep my word when dealing with his kind."

3

The old man's fury was evident in every line of his rigid body. His mouth was twisted still, almost clenched into a knot. The sweat glistered in the deep creases across his temples and the muscles of his arms bunched as though he was about to hurl himself out of his chair. The Egyptian watched, an increasing firmness in the grip on his automatic marking his only concern. A minute passed, and then slowly the old man looked down at the empty gap where his right leg had long ago been removed and his body began to slacken in an admittance of defeat.

The Egyptian glanced towards the manacled son and saw a different type of fury there, more controlled and by its very control more deadly. He moved the automatic to warn the man he called a traitor and turned his head a fraction to call to his two lieutenants who waited outside.

That was when the old man moved, his muscles bunching in one great surging effort. He thrust himself away from his chair by the power of his arms alone and roared to his son to run as he half fell and half threw himself upon the

Egyptian. The officer turned and fired as the encircling arms clamped around his startled neck. The close range impact of the bullet slammed the old one-legged man backwards but his hands still gripped and he dragged the Egyptian with him. They toppled and crashed down with the dying man still embracing his murderer in a bizarre hug. The Egyptian fired again as the old man croaked a second command for his son to flee, and this time the gun was thrusting hard into the dying man's body.

The son was already leaping forwards and his manacled fists slammed down in a titanic two handed blow across the back of the Egyptian's neck. Had he been able to reach the automatic he would have stayed to fight, but the gun was crushed between the bodies of murdered and murderer, and he could hear the Egyptian officer's two lieutenants crashing towards the door.

For a moment he hesitated, and then he ran for the open window. The door opened behind him as he dived through in one flying leap, his knees lifted high and his elbows tucked into his sides to pass through the narrow gap. Two revolvers roared in unison but they were seconds too late.

He hit the ground feet first, rolled forwards and then twisted to his feet again. He ran blindly and turned into the merciful opening of an alley mouth only a few yards away. He ran on with all his strength, twisting and turning until he reached a darkened cul-de-sac over a mile away where he collapsed panting with exhaustion.

He crouched there in the blackness, regaining his breath and fighting down the prickle of emotion that burned the back of his eyes. His face was blurred with shadows of hatred and guilt, and of grief and rage. When he moved on those emotions had been forced back beneath the surface and his face had become a mask, but nothing had been, or ever would be, forgotten.

He hurried through the night and was lost in the gloomy network of streets. He had to get free of his handcuffs, but that was only the start.

1

In the Djemaa El Fina

The watching crowd shuddered with fear and respect as the python's head disappeared into the snake-charmer's mouth. The wild, tattered figure arched his body backwards, his feet splayed apart like those of a limbo dancer and his eyes staring directly behind him from widened sockets. He held the snake's head in his mouth while his right hand gripped it at arm's length half-way along the thickening six-foot body. His two turbanned assistants beat faster at their skin-topped drums as he moved forward with jerky, waddling steps, waving the python's tail in slow circles at his entranced audience.

Alan Ross stood on the fringe of the motley crowd, sweating a little in the still fierce heat. He was just a little taller than average, wearing a dark shirt and faded jeans. Vivid blue eyes clashed with his black hair. At twenty-five he had just finished university and had spent the last two months travelling cheaply through southern Europe before crossing south to Morocco and then down the country to Marrakech.

At first he had found the performers in the famed Djemaa el Fina square slightly disappointing. The wailing notes of the Arab musicians had been tuneless. The little Berber with the monkeys chained to his belt had done nothing more than lead them around in circles while puffing on a wooden flute. The story-tellers and the squatting ancients selling their pills and potions in mysterious twists of paper had merely jabbered expressively in meaningless Arabic. Alan had gazed momentarily at each performer as he moved about the great square, and then he had found the villainous-looking snakecharmer with the python coiled about his arm and a hooded cobra swaying at his feet, and the reputation of Marrakech had been confirmed.

Alan edged deeper into the ring of

spectators as the snakecharmer pulled the python from his mouth with a flourish, shaking his head and jabbering fanatically at the crowd. One of the assistants exchanged his drum for a wooden collection box and a few small coins rattled into it as he paced around the circle.

The snake-charmer returned the python to one of the stout wooden boxes at his feet but continued to shout and gesture at the crowd. Some of the watchers shuffled away, but Alan was content to wait and took the opportunity to glance idly around the cautious circle of spectators as the build-up began again.

Most of them were Moroccans, dark-skinned and wearing the long one-piece djellabahs that reached to their feet. A few of them were hooded but most had pushed the hoods back on to their shoulders and wore a knitted skull cap or a fez. There were a few eagle-nosed Rif from the desert in coarse brown robes like medieval monks, and one wide-eyed Negro holding a bicycle. There was only one other European, a large jovial-faced man wearing a white shirt and grey flannels who looked as though he just had to be English. He was standing almost opposite Alan beside a pock-faced Arab guide in a bright red fez who was apparently making some attempt to translate the snake-man's words.

Alan's attention reverted to the centre of the circle again as the snake-man drew a bashful and only half-willing volunteer from the audience. The turbanned assistants renewed the dramatic throbbing of their drums while the reluctant victim, a bare-headed young Arab wearing a grey and white striped djellabah, took great care to avoid the motionless cobra that watched him with bright, unblinking eyes. The snake-charmer held him by one arm as he paused to launch a fresh volley of spluttering Arabic at the crowd.

The tirade finished and the snake-man turned to his volunteer. There was a solemn ritual of immunising the young Arab by rubbing the backs of his hands and then each of his cheeks against the snake-charmer's forehead, obviously to transfer some of the snake-man's power

10

and protect the volunteer. Finally the two squatted in the centre of the circle and after insistent instructions from his tutor the young Arab placed both hands on the snake-man's shoulders and kissed him on the forehead.

Alan prevented a light smile as he watched the elaborate precautions, and decided that even though he was now ostensibly safe from harm the volunteer still did not look too happy as his benefactor reached for the nearest wooden box. The sliding lid was pushed back and the sleepy head of the python was once more revealed. The snake-charmer lifted his pet clear of the box, made pious incantations to heaven, and then draped it around the neck of his nervous subject.

The young Arab put on a brave face as the thick body coiled around his shoulders, but the python was sluggish and looked almost bored. The Arab looked down at the flat head and made a smile, and then trembled a little as the snake-man slid back the lid on another of the closed wooden boxes. The occupant of this box was thinner and

11

darker, but decidedly more sinister. Alan guessed it to be one of the viper family, and although its venom was undoubtedly drawn he could understand the feelings of the young volunteer. The snake-charmer reassuringly allowed the new snake to crawl around inside his shirt for a few moments and then passed it into his subject's hands. There were more voluble reassurance and instructions, beaming smiles from the snake-man, and then abruptly the snakes were bundled back into their respective boxes and the act was over.

After a vigorous handshake the young Arab returned to his applauding companions in the crowd. The turbanned assistants rattled the collecting boxes again and Alan parted from another coin before starting to move away. Then, even as he turned, he saw the pock-faced guide with the large Englishman on the far side of the circle lower his head in a surreptitious nod towards the snake-charmer.

Alan hesitated. Another second and he would have imagined that the pock-marked man had merely blinked, or moved his head to avoid a fly, and he would have continued on his way. Then the snake-charmer started off again with his insistent coaxing for a volunteer, and this time his out-stretched hand was extended towards the large Englishman.

"Oh no!" The Englishman backed away, raising both hands defensively but grinning at the same time.

Alan stopped and grinned in sympathy, for he could wholly see the big man's point of view. The snakes were clearly harmless, but the unappetising prospect of kissing the snakecharmer as part of the introduction ceremony was enough to make anyone think twice. Apart from his filthy clothes and tangled rat's-tails of flying black hair, the wild-eyed snakeman looked as though he undoubtedly found soap and water as repulsive as most people found his slithering pets.

The Englishman, for Alan had no doubt of his nationality now, continued to protest and shake his head, but the guide beside him was earnestly supporting the snake-charmer, his bright red fez bobbing erratically as he insisted that the ceremony was less involved for a European and with no kissing. Alan watched and saw from the grin on the man's face that he found the challenge tempting and was slowly wavering.

Sensing that the Englishman could be persuaded several of the spectators joined in, urging and cajoling in grinning Arabic. The big man looked round the circle of cheerfully pressing faces and grinned back. Then he shrugged his broad shoulders and allowed the snake-man to take his hand and draw him into the centre of the circle. The applauding crowd shouted more encouragement and then became silent as the snake-charmer began his insistent instructions. As he spluttered and gestured vehemently the pock-faced guide translated clumsily from the edge of the audience.

"He say you must trust — he say you must believe in him. If you have faith the snakes cannot harm you. He ask if you have faith? You must tell him yes or no."

The big man tried to stop grinning and nodded vigorously.

The snake-charmer looked pleased and talked even faster, his hands jerking in wild, expressive movements. Then abruptly he siezed the Englishman's left hand in both his own and rubbed his forehead hard against the back of the wrist. He repeated the movement with the right hand and then gripped the big man's shoulders. The Englishman winced and wrinkled his nose, and the majority of the crowd grinned openly as they rubbed foreheads. The snake-charmer drew back and loosed another stream of Arabic, and again the guide translated.

"He say that you are safe now. The snakes will not harm you. But only if you still believe. If you do not believe you must say so, for the snakes will know."

The Englishman nodded soberly.

"Tell him I believe."

The guide translated and the snake-man beamed again. His hands returned to the big man's shoulders to press him down, and they squatted facing each other on the ground. The assistants beat

15

upon their drums as the snake-man slid back the lid of the box containing the python.

He lifted the reptile out, holding it between them in both hands. His insistent demand was unmistakable now and without waiting for the translation the Englishman nodded affirmatively. The snake-man rubbed the python's flat head against his own greasy cheek, and then reached forward to drape the long coiling body around the Englishman's neck. The big man shuddered slightly as the scaly body touched cold upon his flesh, but smiled almost immediately.

The snake-man reached out for the second box, hesitated, and then passed over it to a third box, as yet unopened. He drew the box towards him and slipped back the lid. His hand dipped swiftly inside and came out holding a second viper close behind the head. Again the fast, demanding spate of words, and again the Englishman inclined his head in a reassuring nod. The snake-man held the slim, deadly-looking viper in both hands now, and he extended both arms and signed to the big man to take it from him.

The Englishman licked his lips, looking faintly apprehensive for the first time. The viper was squirming slightly in the snake-man's hands and looked much livelier than the other reptiles that had been produced. Then perhaps because it was too late to back out now with the whole crowd watching him so closely, the big man slowly reached out and accepted the offered snake.

The snake-charmer drew his hands back and smiled. The Englishman started to relax, and then abruptly the viper twisted into a flash of striking muscle, the forked tongue flickered for the most inestimable fraction of a second and the black head darted straight at the big man's throat.

A black-robed woman screamed behind her veil, drowning the Englishman's gargling cry. The crowd scattered outwards in panic as the big man fell backwards with the deathly ribbon of black still writhing in his hands. For a moment Alan could see nothing through the swirl of people, and then he pushed his way to the front again.

The tattered snake-charmer was on his feet, standing over the Englishman's fallen body. He seemed to hover like some great carrion bird with his feet splayed and arms outstretched, and then he dived one hand in a lightning swift grab at the struggling viper that the Englishman still held to his chest. His fist closed on the reptile close behind the neck and yanked it away.

There was utter confusion of shouting and yelling. The hooded cobra that had coiled tamely on the ground throughout the whole act had recoiled away in fright but one of the snake-man's helpers had promptly trapped it beneath an up-turned basket. Now the two assistants were frantically shouting to calm the crowd, and were beginning to succeed now that the snake-charmer had recaptured the viper.

Alan pushed forward to the fallen man's side, without really knowing what he could do to help. The man was still alive but his face was bloodless and there were two ugly incisions just two inches below his left ear where he had jerked his face away and inadvertently exposed his throat. Little smears of blood were tinged with blue traces of poison.

For a moment Alan simply knelt helplessly on the ground, drawn solely because he was the only other Englishman there amongst the swarm of jostling Moroccans. Then with an effort the big man opened his eyes.

Even in death the jovial grin flickered back for a moment.

"What a bloody silly way to die," he said weakly. "I should have known better." His grey eyes were surprisingly clear but his lower jaw seemed half paralysed and moved stiffly as he tried to phrase another sentence. "Stan always did say I was too much of a ruddy exhibitionist."

His jaw became wholly paralysed then, and deliberately, as though determined to save someone else from the unpleasant task after his death, he closed his eyes.

There was a frantic splutter of Arabic beside Alan's shoulder, and he looked up as the snake-charmer brushed past him. The killer viper had been hastily stuffed back into its box and now there was a small knife with a sharp pointed blade in the snake-man's hand. He crouched over the Englishman with the little blade poised to lance the bite, and then he hesitated. Slowly he pushed one grimy hand inside the big man's shirt, and as he watched Alan knew that the big man was dead.

For a moment he felt a strange sense of loss as he looked down at the still face of the man he had never known. The snake-charmer crouched with his useless knife in his hand, his face expressionless and utterly silent. Then the jabbering around them seemed to be renewed as the crowd drew closer again, and abruptly a Moroccan policeman pushed through the mass of people.

Pandemonium broke out as everybody attempted to explain at once. The snake-man became voluble again, standing up and waving his skinny arms. Alan straightened up and stood by helplessly. He spoke neither Arabic nor French and to him it sounded as though the whole crowd were simply snarling and yelping like fighting dogs rather than talking sanely. The policeman suddenly challenged him with a barrage of questions he couldn't understand and he could only spread his arms vaguely and shake his head. He looked round hopefully for the pock-faced Arab guide in the red fez who had translated for the dead Englishman, but the guide had disappeared.

Two more policemen shouldered through the crowd, and from somewhere a blanket was produced and spread over the dead man. One of the new arrivals made a fresh attempt to engage Alan with questions, talking in rapid French.

Alan repeated '*non parlez-vous français*' as apologetically as possible and appealed for someone who spoke English. No one came forward and the unintelligible jabbering around him gained in volume.

For perhaps ten minutes he stood in the middle of the babbling crowd, and then there was a loud hooting as an ambulance appeared and backed steadily into the gesturing horde. The snake-charmer was still arguing violently with two of the policemen and nobody seemed to notice as two attendants dismounted from the ambulance and unloaded a stretcher. The heavy Englishman was carried into the back and Alan was given a brief respite as the third policeman left him alone for a moment to supervise the operation.

The ambulance drove away and a police car nosed up to take its place. The snake-charmer was still stamping his foot and shouting as the two policemen half helped and half pushed him into the back seat. The man who had tried to question Alan pulled open the front door and made an unmistakable gesture of invitation with his hand.

"*M'sieur. S'il vous plait.*"

Alan could hardly refuse and climbed in beside the driver who gave him a reassuring grin. In the back the snake-charmer had now relapsed into glowering silence between his two escorts. The remaining policeman closed the car door and cleared the crowd away as it began to move.

Once clear of the Djemaa el Fina the car moved swiftly through the wide streets of modern Marrakech, and five minutes later braked outside the police station. The snake-charmer burst into fresh protest as he was hustled out of the car and up the steps, and Alan received a sign to follow. Inside the station there was a brief conference around the duty sergeant's desk and then Alan was led into a small ante-room and left waiting.

Ten minutes passed before he was sent for again, and then he was shown into a larger office. Here a more authoritative looking man sat behind a large desk, beneath the inevitable framed picture of King Hassan of Morocco on the wall behind him. A peaked cap rested on the desk by his elbow and he wore gold bars on the shoulders of his crisp grey shirt. He looked slight, but his dark brown eyes were keenly appraising, and his manners were as smooth as his smile.

He said quietly. "Permit me to introduce myself, I am Inspector Haffard. I must apologise if you have been inconvenienced, and — " he inclined his head " — for the regrettable death of your friend. It was a tragic accident."

Alan felt a sense of relief at finally facing someone who spoke his own language. "I didn't know the man," he explained. "I just happened to be there watching."

Haffard looked surprised. "Then I am sorry you were detained. When you rushed forward to help the man it was assumed that you knew him. Especially as he tried to speak to you."

"He didn't say anything," Alan said. "Except that it was a bloody silly way to die. There was an Arab guide with him though, a man with a pock-marked face. I think he ran off, but perhaps he can help you identify the body if you can find him."

"It will not be necessary." Haffard paused and gestured to a chair facing his desk. "But please sit down, Mr. er — ?"

"Ross." Alan accepted the offer and sat down.

"Mr. Ross." Haffard smiled and

continued. "As I was about to say, it should not be necessary to trace the guide. The dead man was carrying a wallet which identifies him as a Mr. George Dawson, and I think we should be able to find as much from the wallet as we would be able to learn from the guide. Most of them offer their services for a few hours and know nothing about their clients anyway. But perhaps, Mr. Ross, now that you are here, you can tell me what happened as you saw it?"

Alan complied with the request and afterwards Haffard nodded sadly.

"That seems to match with the statements my policemen took down from the other witnesses. The whole affair is very unfortunate."

Alan said bluntly. "But what did the snake-charmer have to say about it?"

Haffard looked up, and then nodded again. "Of course, you do not speak Arabic or French. You do not know what they were saying in the square. It appears that this fool of a snake-charmer has recently engaged a new

25

assistant, and this morning it was left to this new assistant to ensure that the snakes were safe to handle. With the poisonous snakes it is simply a matter of enticing them to bite on a cloth and allowing the cloth to drain off the venom, but somehow this particular snake was overlooked. The snake-charmer insists that it was not his fault, and the assistant has taken fright and fled. I am not sure yet whether the snake-man can be charged with manslaughter by negligence, or whether the assistant can be charged if we can find him. In either case it was a stupidly needless accident that I much regret. It is even worse that it had to happen to an Englishman. Very few tourists can be tempted to actually handle the snakes, and it is terrible that one of them should lose his life this way. It could be bad for the tourist trade of Marrakech. Perhaps that is why Dawson's guide ran away, it would be bad publicity to be connected with a dead client."

Just then the telephone rang on Haffard's desk, and with a murmur of apology the Moroccan Inspector transferred his attention and lifted the receiver. He listened in silence and once or twice his dark head nodded slightly.

Alan could distinguish nothing of the muffled words from the other end of the line and as he waited for Haffard to finish he thought back over their brief conversation. The question of the vanishing guide seemed vaguely significant, and suddenly he remembered the surreptitious exchange of glances between the guide and the snake-charmer immediately before the latter had tempted the now dead Dawson into the limelight. He remembered too that the snake-man had been very careful to grip the killer viper close behind the head when he had lifted it from the box and handed it to the unsuspecting Englishman. It was a precaution that he had not bothered to take when handling the safe viper he had used in the previous act. Alan's mouth became suddenly dry as he wondered for the first time whether it was possible that the snake-man had known that this particular snake had not had its venom drawn.

If so it meant that George Dawson had been murdered.

2

An Unlikely Coincidence

Haffard uttered a crisp word of thanks into the telephone and then returned the receiver to its cradle. He looked across at Alan.

"That was one of my sergeants, Mr. Ross. He's been checking on some of the papers found in the unfortunate Mr. Dawson's wallet, and we now know that he was staying at the hotel Mansour. It's a small hotel in the old medina, not far from the Djemaa el Fina square. I have to go there, so if you wish I can give you a lift back to the square in my car."

Alan hesitated. "Don't you want a written statement or anything?"

Haffard shook his head. "I don't think it is necessary. We know exactly what happened and we have a dozen other witnesses who all saw the incident. You are a tourist and no doubt there are other parts of Morocco that you wish to see. There is no point in detaining you here in Marrakech until the inquest."

Alan still hesitated, his sudden suspicions were very prominent in his mind, but he was realising how very weak they would sound to this slight, brisk Inspector who was so willing to dispose of the matter with a swift brush of his hands. The basis of his suspicions were so completely vague, so possibly a trick of his own imagination, that he was reluctant to speak them aloud. Haffard was still waiting for an answer to his offer of a lift, almost impatiently it seemed, and Alan sensed that he preferred the matter to be closed and glossed over. He had already voiced the fact that Dawson's death could harm Marrakech's thriving tourist trade, and possibly there would be far-reaching recriminations if he failed to handle it correctly.

After a moment Alan decided to say nothing, but at the same time his conscience pricked. He compromised clumsily and said,

"I didn't know the man, but somehow,

it doesn't seem right to just walk away and leave it there. Isn't there anything I can do?"

Haffard smiled and shook his head. "Everything will be taken care of, Mr. Ross. There is really nothing that — " He stopped abruptly and a change of expression came over his face.

Alan waited. For a moment the Inspector stared thoughtfully down at his blotter, then he tapped it sharply with his forefinger as though signifying a decision. He looked up.

"There is perhaps one thing. It is really outside my sphere and possibly I should not suggest it. But if you really feel that you should do something for your countryman — ?"

Alan answered the enquiring gaze in the dark brown eyes and after another second of hesitation Haffard went on.

"I have an unpleasant task to perform. The sergeant who just telephoned informed me that Mr. Dawson was not alone in Marrakech. He has a daughter, a Miss Catherine Dawson, who is also staying at the hotel Mansour. It is my duty to

31

inform this young lady of her father's death."

Haffard began to look apologetic. "Of course I will do anything that is possible to assist the young lady, but you realise that my efforts must at best be limited. However, I think that in the circumstances, alone and bereaved in a strange city where she most probably does not speak the language, Miss Dawson will perhaps appreciate the hand of friendship from someone who is also English. There is nothing that anyone can do for her father, but if you do wish to make some gesture perhaps you can make it to the daughter. No doubt she will return to England within a few days, but until then she may need a friend."

Alan faltered at the unexpected suggestion, and almost wished that he had not spoken. To propose himself as a temporary friend to a complete stranger at a time of mourning could prove to be infinitely embarrassing, and he was not sure that he liked the idea. Even if the unknown Catherine Dawson proved grateful his presence could still be inexpedient. Then he realised that Haffard could be right, and that although in normal surroundings she might prefer to be left alone to weep, here in Marrakech she would need a friend. Either way his conscience would hardly rest now until he had at least made an offer of help.

He said at last, "Thank you, Inspector. I would like to go with you when you break the news."

"I should thank you." Haffard smiled briefly, and then became serious again. He pressed the buzzer on his desk and relayed instructions for his car to be available immediately, and then stood up behind his desk. "I think we should go now, before she learns the sad truth from some garbled source. Hotel staff can be so clumsily tactless."

Alan nodded and rose to his feet as the Moroccan donned his peaked cap and then reached for his jacket. They left the office and by the time they reached the street the car was waiting for them.

They drove in silence back to the Djemaa el Fina. The swarming crowds were still there, but now, instead of forming circles around the performers, they were clustered into close groups, jabbering and gesturing among themselves. Alan guessed that Dawson's death was still the main topic of conversation.

Haffard's driver kept up a steady pressure on the horn button to clear a path ahead of them, and a few minutes later pulled up outside the hotel Mansour. It was a small hotel, but, as Haffard explained, fairly expensive. Its choice location in the narrow, mysterious streets of the old medina gave it an attraction that compensated for its lack of grandeur.

Alan followed Haffard out of the car and into the wide bar that formed the frontage of the two storey hotel. Haffard nodded briefly to the barman and then they mounted the staircase that led up from the left hand side of the room. The hotel foyer was at the top of the staircase and after a word with the clerk behind the reception desk Haffard led the way along a carpeted corridor. He knocked on a door numbered with the figure seven.

They waited, and after a moment the door was opened by a young woman who looked at them with enquiring eyes. She wore a simple, light-weight white dress, relieved by a wide, bright red belt that fastened with an ornate gold buckle in the middle of her slim waist. The dress left her arms and throat coolly bare, and she looked exceedingly fresh despite the sluggish heat of early evening. Her hair was dark and her honey-brown eyes slightly flecked with gold. Her self-confident poise faltered a little as she recognised Haffard's uniform.

Haffard said quietly. "Miss Dawson, I am an Inspector of the police, I am afraid that I have some very bad news for you."

Catherine Dawson seemed to recoil slightly. Before she could answer Haffard added.

"May we come in?"

She nodded and stood to one side as they entered the room. Alan, feeling painfully self-conscious beneath the uncertain look she gave him, carefully closed the door.

Haffard explained what had happened as precisely and gently as possible. Catherine Dawson listened and her body seemed to wither inwardly, as though drained of all feeling and only her soul was whimpering. She closed her eyes and her dark head moved in a shivering negative gesture as she tried not to believe. Haffard took her arm and guided her into a chair. She obeyed the pressure of his hands without any will of her own.

Haffard glanced round the room and his gaze rested on a glass-fronted cabinet on a small table by the window. He nodded towards it and said quietly.

"I think you should find some spirits in there, Mr. Ross. Please see if there is some brandy."

Alan nodded and hurried to the cabinet. As Haffard had surmised it was full of bottles and a neat semi-circle of polished glasses. There was a half full bottle of Martell cognac, and he quickly poured a strong measure into one of the glasses. He crossed the room and gave it to Haffard.

The Moroccan gripped the girl's shoulder and shook her gently.

"Drink this, Miss Dawson. It may help. I cannot tell you how sorry I am about your father."

Catherine Dawson opened her eyes, and now they were wet and swimming. She accepted the proffered glass, sipped and coughed weakly. She coughed again to clear her throat and then made an effort to speak.

"Thank — thank you, Inspector. But George Dawson wasn't my father. He was my uncle. But I was very — very fond of him, just the same."

Halfard said quietly, "Take your time, Miss Dawson. There is no hurry for you to talk."

She nodded, and then sipped again at her brandy. For several minutes there was complete silence as Haffard gave her time to recover from the first shock, and then she looked uncertainly towards Alan.

"This is Mr. Ross," Haffard explained. "He saw the accident and tried to help your uncle. It just so happened that not one of my three policemen who reached the scene could speak English, and thinking that Mr. Ross was a friend of your uncle's they brought him to me. When the tangle was sorted out Mr. Ross thought that if you have no friends in Marrakech perhaps he could be of service."

Alan felt awkward, but said as sincerely as he could, "Perhaps I shouldn't try to intrude, Miss Dawson, but if I can do anything I'll be glad to help."

She said slowly. "You're — you're very kind."

There was another clumsy silence, and then Haffard said,

"If you can give me the necessary names and addresses I can undertake to inform your family in England. If your uncle was married then perhaps it should be left to the widow to decide whether his body should be flown home or not."

"He was married." Catherine blinked hard and took another sip at her brandy before continuing. "My Aunt Jane should have been with him on this trip but she broke her ankle, that's why he invited me along instead."

"Then I will make all the necessary arrangements." Haffard drew a pen and notebook from his pocket, and then nodded encouragingly.

Catherine swallowed hard. "The address is — " she hesitated. "I think I can write it down better than I can talk."

"Of course. If you wish." Haffard gave her the pen and the book and she wrote slowly for a few minutes before handing them back. Haffard read what she had written and nodded. "Thank you, Miss Dawson. Your father and your uncle's wife will both be informed. I will see to everything. There is only the matter of your own return to England, but that you do not have to decide immediately. We can perhaps discuss that tomorrow when you have had more time to get over this tragic shock."

She nodded. "Thank you, Inspector."

Haffard stood up. "And now I am afraid that I must leave you. You understand that I have other duties. If there is anything else that I can do you must let me know."

She nodded again and started to rise.

Haffard held up a hand. "No, don't get up. I can see myself out." He moved over to the door and made a little bow of farewell.

Alan felt uncomfortable. He said, "Perhaps I should leave too. I'll call round first thing tomorrow and see if I can help."

Catherine looked at him, hesitated, and then said, "No, don't go just yet. I think I would rather have someone to talk to."

Haffard smiled and opened the door. He bowed again and then closed it as he went out.

Alan stood in embarrassment in the centre of the room, looking at the girl. Her eyes were still wet, but she had not cried since the first shock when Haffard had broken the news, and for the moment she had her feelings under control.

He said at last, "I'm very sorry it happened."

She blinked hard and then looked at him again. "It's not too bad," she said. "At least, not yet. I was very fond of Uncle George, he was my favourite uncle as a child, but I haven't seen him very much in the past six or seven years, so we were not really as close as we could have been. He only decided to bring me to Morocco as a spur-of-the-moment treat when my Aunt slipped on some steps and broke her ankle." She stopped and stared into her glass for a moment and then finished. "The Inspector said you saw it. I'd like to know exactly what happened."

Alan moved closer. He said, "I think the Inspector explained it very well, Miss Dawson. Your uncle allowed himself to be persuaded into taking part in the snakecharmer's act, but one of the snakes had not been properly drained of its poison. The crowd were urging him on, and I think he must have felt he would be letting the side down if he appeared a bad sport. There was a guide with him, a man with a pock-marked face who was translating the snake-charmer's instructions, but he ran away after the accident."

She nodded. "That would be Achmed. Uncle hired him in Fez and he was travelling with us. I suppose he'll come back later if he isn't too scared." She looked up and added hesitantly, "You don't have to call me Miss Dawson you know — my name's Cathy."

"And I'm Alan."

She smiled briefly. Alan relaxed and felt easier now that the atmosphere had become less formal.

Cathy said, "The Inspector mentioned that my uncle tried to speak to you before he died. What did he say?"

"Only that it was a silly way to die. Then he added something about Stan always said he was too much of an exhibitionist. It wasn't much really. He didn't know me, and I suppose he was just talking for the sake of something to say?"

Cathy nodded slowly. "Stan is my father's name. And father did say that Uncle George's fondness for the lime-light would be his undoing. I don't think though that he ever expected — " She stopped herself abruptly and her knuckles whitened where she still gripped her glass.

Alan waited while she took a long sip

at her brandy to cover her emotions, then he said,

"I don't think he suffered, Cathy. It was all over very fast."

She put the glass down and looked at him.

"I think I want to go out," she said abruptly. "I don't want to just — just sit here and brood in this hotel room. Would you mind just walking with me — anywhere? Just as long as we walk and get away from this room."

Alan said quickly. "Of course I don't mind, if you think it will help."

She stood up. "Thank you. I'll just get something else to wear. I — I won't be a moment." She brushed a hand quickly over her eyes and turned away towards the bedroom.

Alan watched her go, and found himself suddenly glad that George Dawson had been her uncle and not her father. His death had still been a bitter shock to her, but not as much as it would have been had they been really close. He was glad too that she had turned out to be too practical to go distraught with grief.

He judged her to be about twenty-two or three, and as well as feeling a natural sympathy for her he was also beginning to like her.

After a few minutes she came back. Her eyes were dry and she had washed away her make-up, restoring only the rich colour of her lips. She had put on flat, sensible shoes, and now wore a white woollen jacket to cover up her bare shoulders and arms.

She said hesitantly. "Are you sure you really don't mind?"

Alan opened the door for her. "I'm sure. And I think it probably is a good idea to get out rather than to sit here and keep thinking about things."

She gave a little nod and then preceded him into the corridor. He locked the door behind her and pocketed the key. The clerk in the foyer looked up as they approached and spoke sorrowfully in French, wringing his hands in a gesture of distress. Cathy thanked him and after a moment they continued down the stairs.

Alan said. "I didn't realise you spoke French."

She smiled faintly. "I can speak it almost fluently, and a smattering of Spanish as well. But I'm still very glad to be able to talk to someone in English. Do you speak any foreign languages?"

He shook his head. "None at all. I'm an engineering student. Building and Civil engineering. At least," he corrected himself sharply, "I was. I've just finished university with all the necessary qualifications, but as I haven't actually taken up a job yet it's difficult to stop thinking of myself as a student. I could, or should be able to, design you a bridge, or build you a dam, but languages I could never master. I don't seem to have the patience to learn anything like that. I'm happier with measurements and concrete and girders — more practical things."

They had reached the ground floor now and he led her out into the street. To their right the narrow thoroughfare led to the tall square tower of the Koutoubia mosque and the Djemaa el Fina, but it seemed unnecessarily tactless to lead her that way. He turned left into the zig-zag

45

maze of the medina, the old quarter of Marrakech.

Cathy said. "Keep talking, please. It helps me not to think. Tell me how you came to Morocco."

Alan smiled. "I came by a combination of buses, trains, and plain old-fashioned hitch-hiking. I started off a couple of months ago because it seemed likely to be the last chance I would get to spend any real length of time in Europe before taking up a regular job. I went through France and Switzerland, down into Italy, and then back through France again and into Spain. Finally I decided I could just afford to take in a little of North Africa as well so I crossed the straits to Morocco."

Alan continued to talk as they walked slowly through the twisting, badly-surfaced streets, describing his travels and anything else that would help to take her mind off her loss. A constant swirl of people pushed past them, hooded men with suspicious eyes and trailing robes, bare-legged youths bouncing erratically on ancient pedal cycles, donkey carts and donkey riders, yelling the endless, "Balek! Balek!" ("Make way! Make way!") and the hurrying women, some with babies slung upon their backs, completely hidden but for the narrow slit above the veil that revealed dark, lustrous, always curious eyes. The fascination of the people was another asset in the circumstances, and so was the endless interest of their surroundings. The night sky was velvet black through the gaps among the stretches of rush-matting, close-knitted bullboos or sagging strips of balooning sacking that covered over the narrow streets. The cramped shops, hung with silks and carpets were full of light and a riot of colour, and the constant clutching hands and cries of, "Come see! Come see!", from the proprietors provided an almost irresistible diversion from any morbid train of thought.

Then, after an hour of aimless walking, Cathy suddenly said,

"Alan, could we — could we walk somewhere more quieter. I still don't want to face the emptiness of that hotel room. But I've seen enough of all this

47

life and bustle. Normally, I'd enjoy it, but tonight it seems callous even to stay here when my uncle has just died."

Alan gave a nod of understanding and took her arm. "All right," he said. "If I can find my way out, I will."

He had a hazy sense of his direction and led her away from the more commercial centre of the old town. The streets became narrower, darker and more sinister. The close walls seemed unnaturally high, although they only rose to two storeys, and there were a host of strange smells and only an occasional passer-by. From behind a massive, bolt-studded door with a huge iron ring latch came the unnerving sound of high, shrill Arab music.

Then at last they came to a high, solid wall, the outer ramparts of Marrakech. They walked along in its shadow for perhaps seventy yards and then passed through a high, arched gateway. Outside the old city the mighty, rust-brown walls stretched away on either side, the monotony broken by buttressing towers and clumps of date palms. Ahead stretched a barren plain, and far away, unseen in the night, were the outlines of the rugged Atlas mountains.

Alan said quietly, "We can walk along the walls. If we turn right we shall be moving back towards the hotel, if we turn left we shall be moving farther away."

"Left," Cathy said, realising that the choice was hers. "It's so still and peaceful out here. I'd like to walk a little farther."

She became silent as they walked side by side along the outer ramparts, and Alan spoke solely to drive away her thoughts.

"I've told you how I came to Marrakech," he said. "Now you can tell your story."

She smiled faintly. "I've told you some of it. I came here because Uncle George invited me. He was researching for a book on the background history of Morocco, he'd already written similar books on Spain and Italy. We drove through France and Spain practically non-stop, because he wanted to spend as much time as possible here in Morocco."

She talked, almost absent-mindedly,

of the ferry crossing from Algeciras to Tangier, and as he listened Alan's attention wandered slowly along the silhouette of the ancient walls. The star-filled backcloth of the night sky gave them a sinister beauty and threw dark, squared shadows across the bare earth. The spreading fronds of the slender palms brushed against the night and there was the soft murmur of crickets. Cathy talked on quietly and Alan brought his gaze slowly back to the section of the wall immediately above them, and then he stiffened as a movement broke the still outline on top of the ramparts.

Alan moved with an instinct as old and frightening as time, springing at Cathy and knocking her flying out of the way. In the same second part of the ramparts seemed to rush towards them and there was a crash that trembled the earth as a giant section of crumbling masonry hit the spot where they had stood just one second ago. A shower of falling stones trickled down and they were enveloped in a shower of dust.

Alan lay on one side, his arm protectively

braced across Cathy's shoulders as she choked beside him. He craned his neck to stare up at the now empty section of the wall and slowly realised that the possibility of that narrow escape being another accident after his suspicion about Dawson's death would make a very unlikely coincidence.

3

The Road to Casablanca

Alan got up slowly and helped Cathy to
her feet. She was still coughing from the
settling dust and stared in horror at the
jagged, knee-high lump of broken red
sandstone rock beside her. Alan could
feel her arms trembling under his hands
as he steadied her and there was still a
trace of panic in the jerky movement of
her breasts.

"Are you all right?" he demanded
sharply.

"I — I think so."

She was very unsure and couldn't quite
pull her eyes away from the slab of wall
that had missed them so narrowly.

Alan's gaze still searched the top of the
ramparts.

"Stay here," he said. "And don't go
too close to the wall."

He released her and she stared after

him, breathing painfully. He moved swiftly along the wall to the nearest towerlike buttress, stared upwards for a moment, and then began to climb. There were many cracks and fissures in the red sandstone and he moved up with ease. His mouth, which she was unable to see, was clenched tight and he was savagely angry.

The great wall was at this point at least twenty foot high, but Alan gave no thought to falling as he scaled it with swift, scrambling movements. He neared the top and got both hands over the edge. Here he hesitated for a moment, suddenly realising how easy it would be for anyone to kick him in the face and knock him clear off the wall as he pulled his head over, and then anger spurred him again and he heaved himself up.

There was no one on the flat top of the square buttress tower, and no one anywhere in sight along the top of the wall. Alan balanced on the edge, his palms on the wall and his arms stiff, and then he rolled himself forward and brought his legs up. A moment later he was standing upright.

He glanced down at Cathy who still remained where he had left her, staring up at him with a perplexed expression on her face. Then he moved warily along the top of the wall. He reached the jagged gap where the slab of sandstone had broken away, but there was still nothing to be seen.

Alan moved to the inner edge of the wall and looked down into the narrow street below. It was empty. Across the gap stretched the flat roof-tops of the medina, most of them slightly lower than the crenellated walls, and few of them on the same level. The towers of the mosques broke up the nonconformity even more, and far to the left was the larger, dominating tower of the koutoubia. Below was darkness and an almost tense silence, and black, narrow alleyways leading off from the street that ran inside the wall.

Alan stared at those black openings and realised that in the time that he had taken to climb the wall another man could just as swiftly have descended on the inside and vanished. If there had been another man?

He returned to the broken gap in the wall. There were several cracks in the sandstone around it and another large slab seemed on the point of breaking away. There was nothing to show whether the original fall could have been man-made or not, but Alan had an almost certain feeling that it had not been an accident.

He looked down at Cathy and waved her away. When she had backed up he dislodged the remaining loose sections of the wall to prevent any genuine accidents later, and then made his way back to the point where he had climbed up. His anger receded as he began the descent and when he dropped to the ground again he was able to face Cathy with a reassuring smile on his face.

She came towards him slowly, her expression still uncertain.

"Alan, what's wrong? Why did you have to go climbing up there?"

He hesitated, reluctant to alarm her. "I had to push the rest of that loose stuff down," he said at last. "It might have fallen on someone else."

"But you were looking down the inside of the wall. What were you looking for?"

"Nothing," he said weakly. "It was just — just an interesting view, that's all. You can see right across the roof-tops of the medina." He took her arm and went on urgently. "I think we'd better go back to the hotel — now."

Cathy was still shaken, but she held her ground. The starlight seemed to reflect the gold flecks in the honey-brown eyes to give them a bright, searching quality. She said slowly,

"Alan you didn't believe that fall was an accident — did you?"

There was no point in any further evasion. He said bluntly.

"No, Cathy, I didn't. And I still don't. Now let's go back to your hotel."

She seemed on the point of arguing further, and then changed her mind and remained silent. Alan smiled approvingly and still held her arm as they returned the way they had come, but this time he

56

steered her well clear of the ramparts.

Some of the beauty had gone out of the night now, and the high walls seemed more menacing and ageless than before. A cool wind began to blow in from the Atlas ranges, and the air held a definite chill.

They reached the arched gateway through which they had passed before, but Alan ignored it and continued along the outside of the wall. He no longer fancied the prospect of returning through the dark, twisting alleyways, many of them leading into dead ends. Cathy looked at him strangely, but accepted his leadership without comment.

It was a long walk, but at last they came to a complete break in the walls where a wide, main road drove straight in towards the Djemaa el Fina. A large, illuminated fountain played in the centre of the entrance and when they turned in towards the city the rising tower of the Koutoubia was directly ahead of them. The tower was flood-lit, and that and the fountain behind them provided a more civilised touch that made Alan feel ensier as he guided the girl back to the main square and then to her hotel.

They had walked almost in silence since leaving the scene of their narrow escape but once back in her hotel room Cathy became resolute again and demanded an explanation.

Alan evaded her questions and her eyes. For the last half hour he had been trying to decide how much he ought to tell her, or whether he should tell her anything at all, and he still hadn't made up his mind. It would be so terribly wrong to distress her with his suspicions if they should prove to be false.

At last he said, "Cathy, I think you should go back to England as soon as possible. Now that your uncle is dead it isn't — " he almost said safe, but changed it at the last moment, "it isn't right for you to stay on alone in Marrakech."

Cathy watched him but didn't answer.

He rushed on hopefully. "You could fly out first thing tomorrow. If you speak to Haffard he's bound to ensure you a seat on the first available plane. He promised any help he could give."

Cathy said slowly. "I can't rush off and leave everything just like that. There's all Uncle's luggage and the car. I had thought about driving home, but I don't have an international licence for Morocco. I don't know how long it will take to get one."

Alan hesitated, then said impulsively, "Then let me drive you, I've got an international licence. Back home it's just a matter of applying to the A.A. or R.A.C., providing you already hold a British licence."

"But I couldn't ask you to do that and ruin your holiday."

"My holiday is over. I have to start back for England within a day or so anyway." He smiled and added, "You'll be helping me as much as I help you, I need the lift."

Cathy moved over to a chair by the wall and sat down slowly and deliberately, without taking her eyes from his face.

"It's a generous offer," she said quietly. "And I'll consider it — after you've told me why you're so suddenly eager to get me out of Marrakech. You acted as

59

though that wall had been deliberately pushed down on us. Why would anybody want to do that?"

He hesitated, and then faced her squarely.

"Possibly because someone wanted to kill you."

She flinched, but after a moment her face was calm again.

"Why should anybody want to kill me?"

It was too late to be anything but frank. He answered quietly.

"Why should anyone want to kill your uncle? The reasons are probably the same."

Her composure shattered and she jerked upright, her fingers digging hard into the arms of her chair. Her eyes were wide and she swallowed hard.

"But — but that was an accident. The Inspector said so. *You said so!* You saw it. It happened in front of a whole crowd of witnesses."

"Cathy, I'm sorry." He moved impulsively closer and his hand touched her shoulder. "I shouldn't have told you.

I should have spoken to Haffard. But it was all so — so vague. Even now I'm not certain."

Cathy's face had paled, and for a moment she was unable to answer as she struggled to adjust herself to the new shock. Then she looked up into his face, searching for relief but finding that he was still quiet and serious. Finally she said,

"Sit down, Alan. Please. And tell me why you think my uncle's death was — wasn't an accident."

Alan pulled up a chair and sat down facing her.

"There were several reasons," he began slowly. "The first was the guide. The man you called Achmed. I'm sure there was a nod, a sort of look of understanding between him and the snake-charmer, before your uncle was persuaded to step forward. And it was Achmed who insisted on pushing him out there, and afterwards Achmed was the first one to vanish.

"Then there was the snake-charmer's act. I saw him perform it with an Arab volunteer before your uncle stepped forward, and there were too many differences. With the Arab the snake-man took a snake from it's box, he held it quite loosely and carelessly, and he allowed it to wriggle around inside his own shirt to prove that it was quite harmless before he handed it to the volunteer. Yet when he did the same act with your uncle, the snake-man deliberately passed over the safe snake he had used the first time, and took an exactly similar snake from a second box, a box that hadn't been opened before. And this time he grabbed the snake quickly and made sure that he held it close behind the head so that it couldn't twist and strike back. He didn't follow the pattern of pushing it inside his shirt and letting it crawl round his waist, but simply handed it straight over to your uncle."

He paused and then finished. "I think the snake-charmer knew that second snake was still full of venom. I think your uncle was murdered."

Cathy's face was still pale and her hands were still gripping tightly to the arms of her chair. Without consciously thinking Alan covered one of her hands with his own, gently but firmly until she relaxed.

She said slowly, "Why didn't you tell this to Haffard?"

"Because I wasn't sure. I don't suppose I would have noticed that the snake-charmer hadn't followed the pattern of his previous act, or at least would have thought nothing of it, if I hadn't seen that exchange of glances with Achmed. And I couldn't actually swear that there was any signal between them, it was so brief. And even if I had said anything to Haffard, I don't think he would have believed me. Or else he wouldn't have wanted to believe me. He's worried about the effect of the matter on the tourist trade and wants the whole thing over and settled as quickly and quietly as possible. The whole thing would have sounded so imaginative that I wouldn't have expected anyone to believe it anyway. But that wall falling down, or being pushed down, has made me think again. I can't believe that it was coincidence."

Cathy closed her eyes and pressed one hand across her forehead.

"It just doesn't seem possible. There's no reason."

"There must be a reason somewhere. Your uncle must have had enemies. Perhaps he had visited Morocco before."

She lowered her hand and shook her head.

"No. This was the first time he had ever visited North Africa. All his previous travels were in Europe. Besides, he was too kind and cheerful. He wasn't the sort to make enemies."

"But he must have had at least one. You must both have the same enemy, because that second accident was meant for you."

She faltered for a moment, and then said, "I'm not sure about that, Alan. I can't think why anyone could possibly want to kill me. But a lot of people must have seen him speak to you when he died, and they didn't speak English to understand what he was saying. Someone, perhaps the snake-man or one of his assistants, may have thought that he was passing some kind of message to you, something that may have been important.

And you were right beside me when that wall fell. If it wasn't an accident then it was more than likely intended for you."

Alan stared at her, and felt a sudden chill brushing the base of his spine.

"I hadn't thought of that," he admitted slowly.

They were silent for several moments, and then Cathy asked,

"What are you going to do?"

Alan looked at her blankly. "I don't know. I still don't think my story is strong enough to convince Haffard, even if he was willing to be convinced. That wall could have been an accident, and I could find nothing to prove otherwise. And as for your uncle, that exchange of glances between Achmed and the snake-man could have been my imagination and I couldn't honestly swear that it wasn't. If only we could find some motive for your uncle to be murdered it would help, without that I think Haffard would probably laugh me out of his office."

Cathy's brow furrowed, but after a moment she again shook her head.

"There is no motive," she said helplessly.

Alan straightened up slowly, watching her, and wishing that he had not put his hazy suspicions into words.

"All right," he said. "Perhaps I was wrong. But even so I think you ought to get out of Marrakech — get right out of Morocco. There's no point in taking any unnecessary risks."

Cathy touched her forehead again and winced.

"No, Alan, I can't just walk away from it as easily as that." She closed her eyes for a moment and then opened them again. "Alan, I'm very grateful for the way you've helped me, and I don't want to sound all weak and womanish, but can we stop talking about it until tomorrow. Right now I've got the most awful headache and I just can't think straight."

"I'm sorry." He was embarrassed. "I didn't realise."

She put a hand on his arm and forced a smile. "It's all right, and I really am grateful. I'll take some tablets and try to get some sleep, then tomorrow I should be able to decide things better and we can go through Uncle's papers and notes and try to find some kind of motive." She hesitated. "I — I've got no right really — to expect you to come back, I mean — but you will won't you."

"Of course I will."

"Thank you." Her temples creased with pain, and then she went on, "It is getting late anyway, it's almost midnight."

Alan felt a sudden wave of concern.

"I'm not sure whether I should leave you," he said. "Not after what happened tonight."

She smiled faintly. "I'll be all right. No one will try to harm me here in the hotel. But what about you? You have to go out in the streets again back to — back to where?"

He smiled in return. "Back to another hotel. It's a little smaller and a little cheaper than this one. But I'm quite capable on my own, and it's only fifty yards or so on the other side of the Djemaa el Fina."

She still looked worried and said

earnestly, "You will be careful, won't you."

Alan nodded reassuringly and stood up to take his leave.

★ ★ ★

When he returned the next morning Cathy was already up, despite the early hour. She opened the door wearing a fresh black skirt and a short-sleeved, orange-coloured blouse. They greeted each other with the awkwardness of new acquaintances and Alan felt very self-conscious of his faded jeans and yesterday's shirt as she invited him in. She assured him that he wasn't too early, and that she was feeling much better after a night's sleep, then there was an awkward pause.

Cathy filled the pause by offering him coffee from the silver tray that had been brought in to her just before his arrival. Then, when they were settled, she said frankly,

"Alan, I said last night that this morning I would decide what I wanted

68

to do — well I think I've decided."

Alan lowered his coffee. "Go on," he encouraged.

"Well, after you'd left I took some tablets, but I still couldn't sleep. I just couldn't stop thinking about poor Uncle George, and your suspicion that he might have been murdered. So eventually I got up and went to his room to check through all his notes. I found nothing, but there were several addresses of people he'd talked to in Fez, Meknes and Casablanca while researching for his book."

She stopped, then began again. "Alan, if he was murdered then the answers must be here in Morocco, and I can't go home without making some attempt to find out the truth. And the only way that I can think of to find out the truth is to go right back to the beginning and retrace the route we followed through Morocco, and talk to all those people that Uncle consulted for material before he died. It should only take a few days. There's a man in Casablanca where we started, and two others in Fez with whom Uncle spent a lot of time. I wanted to talk to them, and then if I can find some hint of a motive for murder I'll come back to Marrakech and tell everything we know to Inspector Haffard."

She looked at him hopefully. "Alan, you offered to drive me home to England last night. Will you drive me now to Casablanca?"

Alan thought it over, but he couldn't refuse. He simply nodded and gripped her hand on it.

★ ★ ★

An hour later they had both packed and checked out of their respective hotels, and Alan had taken George Dawson's place behind the wheel of a brand new, dark-green Ford Zephyr. His single large rucksack containing his belongings and spare clothes was propped on the wide back seat, and Cathy sat upright but silent beside him, the breeze rustling her dark hair through the open windows. They had left a message for Haffard with the manager of the Mansour hotel, telling the Moroccan Inspector that Alan was simply taking Cathy to stay with friends until the question of whether Dawson should be buried locally or flown back to England had been decided.

They drove out of Marrakech and through the great palm groves that surrounded the Casablanca road. The bright sun was fierce on the red earth, and the countless palm fronds swayed like lethargic feather dusters against the harsh blue sky.

4

A Knife in the Medina

Alan completed two and a half hours of fast driving before reaching the last stretch of the hundred and fifty mile journey to Casablanca and then at last they saw the city and the broad sweep of the Atlantic below them as they breasted the rise of a hill. From here Casablanca was a vast, dusty maze, the skyline broken by the tall derricks of the dockside and the mushrooming glass and concrete skyscrapers that marked the wide boulevards of the commercial centre. They had made their plans during the drive, and as he drove the Zephyr into the city Alan followed Cathy's directions to a small hotel, the Siroco, which she knew from her previous stay. There they booked separate rooms and deposited their luggage before returning to the car.

Cathy studied a large, loose-leaved notebook that had belonged to George Dawson and read quietly.

"General Emile Laurand. The villa Menara on the boulevard Moulay Abbas. That's out towards Mohammedia." She looked up. "My uncle spent most of his time in Casablanca with the General. The old man served with the French Foreign Legion during the Rif insurrection of 1921 to 26, and he knows more about that period of Moroccan history, and the history of the French in Morocco than anyone else. He's retired now and in his late seventies, but he gave Uncle a lot of help."

"Then the General shall be our first stop." Alan eased in the gear lever and clutch and the large, dark-green car pulled smoothly towards the centre of the road.

They drove back through the wide, palm-lined boulevards beneath the white skyscrapers, and then gradually left the modern buildings behind as they neared the outskirts of the city. Cathy gave directions to the boulevard Moulay Abbas and at last they found the villa Menara, one of a line of smart modern buildings shaded by palms and flanked by gardens of prickly cactus and flowering shrubs.

They left the car and Alan opened the ornamental iron gates that gave access to the villa. Cathy led the way up the crazy paving path and he followed a few steps behind her. They reached the columned porch, but before they could ring the bell a Moroccan manservant appeared through the glass-panelled doors.

The man's teeth flashed in a smile of recognition and his fez bobbed in a brief bow. Cathy spoke to him in French and his fez bobbed affirmatively as he invited them in. His hands moved like fluttering brown birds as he spoke to Cathy and then he hurried away.

Cathy turned to Alan and interrupted his idle appraisal of the room.

"Laurand is at home," she said. "The manservant has gone to tell him we are here."

After a few moments the general appeared, a white-haired old man who looked less than his seventy odd years.

He was not very tall, and would have looked smaller still had it not been for the erect, military bearing that still remained in his braced shoulders. His face was dark and weathered, and clashed strongly with a clipped white moustache. He hurried towards Cathy and gripped her hand in both his own with the impulsive sincerity of a true Frenchman.

"Mademoiselle Catherine — " The rest of his words were completely lost upon Alan, but Cathy understood and nodded quietly.

"Thank you, General. I should have realised that my uncle's death would be in this morning's paper. The fact that you already know what has happened saves me a painful explanation."

Laurand offered more words of consolation, then as soon as she could Cathy introduced Alan.

"This is Mr. Ross, he's been very kind to me and drove my car here from Marrakech. He doesn't speak French, but I know you speak excellent English."

Laurand extended a hand. "I am glad to know you, Monsieur. Please pardon my unintended rudeness in speaking a language you do not understand."

Alan mumbled a suitable reply and then Laurand turned back to Cathy.

"But tell me, Mademoiselle, why have you returned here to Casablanca? How can I help you in your grief?"

Cathy hesitated, no longer confident of the story she and Alan had agreed upon during the drive from Marrakech, for they had decided to say absolutely nothing of their suspicions until they could support them with something more factual. Then she drew a breath and said,

"It's very simple, General. My uncle's research was almost complete, and it is only a matter of putting his notes in order and his book is practically written. I worked with him, acting as his secretary, and I know how much publishing this book meant to him. It seems terrible that all his work should be wasted, so I feel that the least I can do for his memory is to finish the manuscript for him. I was hoping that you would be so kind as to briefly go over the basis of your conversations with him so that

I can be perfectly sure that I understand his notes properly." She smiled faintly. "Some of his handwriting is very hurried and scribblish, and I don't want to make any mistakes."

Laurand's keen grey eyes never once left her face as she spoke, and when she had finished he was silent for a moment.

"I suspect that your uncle's work was not as near completion as you would have me believe," he said at last. "But that only gives me more respect for you and the task you are undertaking. It takes courage to attempt something so practical for a man's memory, and I think your uncle would appreciate the gesture more than tears. Of course I shall do everything possible to help you."

He took her hand again. "Come, Mademoiselle. I will order Aziz to bring some coffee and refreshment, and you shall ask me anything you wish." He looked to Alan for a moment. "You too, Mr. Ross, will you join us please."

Alan thanked him and followed as he led Cathy into a comfortable study filled with sunlight from a large bay window that took up the whole of one end of the room. The walls were covered with leather-bound books and hung with framed and faded maps of Morocco, Algeria and the Sahara. An ancient, silver-embossed flint-lock musket hung above two curved Arab knives, and beside them hung the kepi of an officer of the Legion. Laurand waved his two guests into two of the three roomy leather armchairs, which with an oak writing-desk comprised the only furniture, and called to the manservant as he drew the curtains to shut out the blinding sunlight.

When the silent Aziz had received his instructions Laurand seated himself facing them in the remaining armchair and raised his eyebrows enquiringly.

"Now, my friends, what do you wish to know."

Cathy said tentatively, "Well, if you could just review briefly the conversations in which my uncle showed most interest."

Laurand smiled. "Beware, Mademoiselle. Put an old soldier on his favourite

78

hobby-horse and he will ride you to the ground. Your uncle was interested in the complete history of the French army in Morocco. As you undoubtedly know French intervention in this country began back in 1900 when marauding tribesmen looked upon it as a refuge after making raids over the border into Algeria which we already controlled. I first served in the Legion under General Lyautey in 1911. I was a green lieutenant then, only twenty-two years old. I was with the expedition that was landed north of Rabat, and fought with them for three years until we eventually cut through the country to link up with our armies in Algeria to create what was known as the Taza corridor, it brought the cities of Meknes, Fez and Taza under our control."

Aziz appeared with the coffee and a tray of sweet cakes, and Laurand signed to him to serve as he continued his story.

"Our activities were curtailed in Morocco almost as soon as we had linked up with our Algerian troops, for so many of our legionaires were drafted to Europe to fight in the First World War. But I was one of the few to stay on in Morocco under Lyautey. There were plenty of skirmishes to keep a young lieutenant on his toes, and the General was a man under whom I was proud to serve.

"When the war in Europe was over Lyautey still did not get the troops he needed for Morocco, and he held the French protectorate with little more than the Legion. Even so he managed to extend the area of French control, but more by diplomacy than actual warfare. Then, in 1921 when I was a captain, the Rif insurrection began, Abd-el-Krim the Rif chieftain gathered a few hundred tribesmen and attacked the outpost of Anual in the Spanish protectorate. The Rif butchered the Spanish garrison and Abd-el-Krim was swift to follow up his advantage as the tribes rose from the mountains to answer his call to arms. The next five years saw the bloodiest war North Africa had ever known. The Rif were fanatical Moslems and the cruellest fighters the Legion ever encountered. Their prisoners were given to the women who were even more vilely cruel than the men. Many a legionaire rifleman risked death himself to creep close enough to a Rif stronghold to put a captured comrade out of his misery."

Laurand paused to sip his coffee and Alan and Cathy waited for him to go on.

"In the finish France and Spain had to join forces to crush the uprising, and in 1925 we launched a wide-scale offensive. By then most of the Legion blockhouses in our hard-won Taza corridor had been stormed by the tribesmen, but one by one, over a series of bloody battles, we took them back. In 1926 Abd-el-Krim was forced to surrender and sent into exile. He died only a few years ago in Cairo." Laurand looked up. "Of course there were more battles after his surrender, for few of his tribes would give up without one last ditch battle, but without Abd-el-Krim the rebellion's back was broken. I gained my promotion to major about that time. It took the Second World War to make me a general."

There was a moment of silence, then Cathy said,

"Thank you, General Laurand. What you have just told me makes me confident that I have got my uncle's notes in the right order, some of the dates were a little vague. But was there anything — anything in which my uncle showed any special interest?"

Laurand frowned. "I do not think so. He was deeply interested in the Rif rebellion, but as that is such a basic part of Morocco's history you must have realised that. He was intending to consult an old Arab chieftain who now lives in Fez, a man named Abd-el-Zeba. El-Zeba is even older than I, and he was one of Abd-el-Krim's lieutenants during the rising. Your uncle wanted a first-hand account of both sides of the story."

Cathy nodded. "I recall that he did spend some time with this man in Fez." She hesitated. "If Uncle was so interested in that period, could you expand a little on the things you told him?"

Laurand smiled. "There are things we talked of that you would not wish to hear. There was nothing romantic about fighting the Rif, they were a cruel people and their favourite trick was to emasculate a man before they butchered him. Such stories your uncle felt were best glossed over even for his book."

He smiled again and patted the arm of his chair. "Come, Mademoiselle. Sit here, and with your permission we will together turn the pages of your uncle's notes, and anything he has written of our interviews that is obscure to you, I will explain."

Cathy hesitated, glancing down at the notebook in her lap to which she had frequently referred. Then she smiled quickly and accepted Laurand's invitation.

For the next half-hour she looked over the white-haired General's shoulder as he slowly turned the pages of Dawson's notes. The old man made frequent comments where the writing was hasty and vague, but to Alan, who was listening carefully, it all sounded completely unhelpful. He just couldn't visualise a motive for murder in a dead rebellion of forty years ago.

At last Laurand closed the book and

looked up into Cathy's face. He said simply,

"And that is the finish, Mademoiselle. The last page of my conversations with your uncle. I hope everything is clear."

Cathy smiled gratefully. "Very clear. You've been most helpful. I'm sure I can write the story now exactly as my uncle intended it to be written." She hesitated. "But there is just one thing — "

She leaned forward to reopen the notebook that rested on Laurand's knee. "This entry here, the numbers and map directions, what do they represent?"

Laurand hunched his head forward for a second and then straightened up. "But of course, they are Legion blockhouses, or forts if you prefer to call them that. Most of them are lost to the desert now, but there are a few crumbling remains. The ruins of blockhouse 9 and blockhouse 17 can still be seen in the Taza corridor. While there are still remains of block-house 38 in the desert south of the Atlas. Your uncle spoke of visiting at least one of them, he thought that a nostalgic word-picture of a ruined desert fort at sunset would make a suitable finish for his book. I gave him the only locations I know and he scribbled them down."

The old man continued to talk, but now that they had been through Dawson's notes page by page Cathy had little excuse to continue probing, and at last she stood up to thank him finally. Laurand rose with her, becoming sympathetic again in consoling her loss and assuring her of any further help she might need. He shook hands firmly and warmly with them both and walked with them as far as his gate.

When they had left the villa behind Alan turned to Cathy and said quietly,

"The General was a wonderful storyteller, but I couldn't see anything in what he told us that might provide a clue to your uncle's death — could you?"

Cathy frowned and slowly shook her head.

Alan pulled the Zephyr's nose out to avoid a donkey cart and then swung back to the right again, he was driving slowly because there was no point in hurrying until he knew where they were going.

Cathy said at last, "The only thing to do is to keep on trying. Uncle spent some time in the museum and the library, so perhaps someone there will remember him, and anything that aroused his special interest. Drive back to the hotel, Alan, and we can leave the car there while we walk round. It's all pretty central."

★ ★ ★

Four hours later they had still learned nothing that would help them in their search for a motive. They had visited both the library and the museum, but nothing had emerged that did not fit the pattern of an ordinary writer researching for historical notes and background material. The respective curators had remembered George Dawson's visits, but that was all. They were both tired and it seemed that their investigations in Casablanca had reached a dead end.

They walked wearily towards the hotel Siroco, and their route led them through the old medina that lay between the modern centre and the sea. The roads here were wider than the alleyways of Marrakech, cobbled and open to the sky. But the mysterious swirls of people were the same, the men hooded and the women veiled.

Alan held Cathy's arm as they walked, to prevent them from getting separated. He said vaguely,

"Is there anything that we might have missed? Any entries among his notes that won't fit with the rest of his research?"

Cathy thought, but ultimately had to shake her head.

"Nothing at all. There are a lot of entries that we won't be able to trace or explain, because he spoke to so many odd people in the street. He would talk to anyone, waiters, policemen, beggars — anyone who was willing to talk to him. Just to enlarge his general background knowledge of the country. He even talked to the pimps and hustlers who wanted to sell him dope or take him to the brothels. But all his notes still tie up with his book."

Alan stopped her for a moment. "You mentioned dope. I've met the sly little men who tap your arm in the medina and offer to sell you marijuana. Could your uncle possibly have quizzed some pimp too closely about his source of supply and become dangerous that way?"

"It's possible," Cathy admitted reluctantly. "But Uncle had too much sense to pry into that sort of thing. His books dealt with history and facts. He tried to avoid sensational disclosures."

They turned into a slightly narrower street that led to their hotel and Cathy went on,

"Uncle George wrote his travel books for adults, but he always claimed that they were equally fit for schoolboys. He would mention dope if it was part of the background, but he wouldn't dig into that sort of aspect."

"Nevertheless, he must have dug into something — "

Alan broke off as a wide donkey cart trundled towards them, jamming indignant passers-by close to the open shop-fronts and walls. Beside them was a wide door providing a brief recession and he moved Cathy into it. They stood side by side with their backs pressed to the scarred, bolt-studded woodwork as the the donkey cart clattered past, the Arab on the cart grinning widely.

"As I was about to say — " Alan began again.

And in that moment a slim, swift figure in a hooded grey djellabah moved out of the alleyway directly opposite. A flash of silver zipped from the extended fingers of the man's lunging arm and blurred past their eyes.

The quivering throwing-knife thudded into the door directly between their heads.

5

The Spin of a Coin

For a moment the knife-thrower seemed frozen in the dark mouth of the alleyway, his body poised on one foot and his arm still thrust forward in the act of releasing the knife. Alan saw a dark, ageless face beneath the hood of the grey djellabah, the mouth barely distinguishable and the eyes bright as sharpened steel. And then the man twisted and was gone.

The tail end of the donkey cart still pinned Alan against the doorway, and for a second he was only conscious of the slender, gleaming blade strumming beside his head, and Cathy's wide, frightened eyes. Then the cart was past and the way ahead was clear, and with a shout to Cathy to stay where she was he plunged into the alley mouth after their attacker.

There was nothing but the high walls and a shadow-filled archway directly ahead, and then at the far end of the gloomy arch Alan saw a flash of grey as the man in the djellabah dodged swiftly round a corner. Alan sprinted furiously, slipped on a mess of rotted fruit as he ducked through the archway, and almost fell round the corner in time to see the grey robe diving into the flowing river of people crossing a main intersection fifty yards away.

With an angry yell Alan spurted up the alley and crashed bodily into the startled Arabs shuffling along the main street. A veiled woman screeched and a shop owner yelled indignantly as his wares were spilled, but Alan raced on without a pause. He could see the grey hood through the heads of the crowd and knew that if he didn't catch the man fast he would lose him.

The whole street was ringing with yells and curses as first the knife-thrower and then the pursuing Alan totally disrupted the flow of commerce. Alan attempted to plough straight through a flock of customers around a crude brazier where a little Berber cooked shish-kebabs of meat on long skewers and lost valuable moments while he shook himself free of the enraged and waving arms. He craned his head as he raced on but the grey djellabah was out of sight.

Alan put on a fresh spurt, but a bucking donkey, frightened by his quarry, suddenly pitched its spluttering rider full into his path and he lost more ground as he stumbled and dodged to avoid tripping. A moment later he reached a minor cross-roads in the narrow street and jerked breathlessly to a stop.

Ahead and on both sides the street was full of jostling Arabs, but the gap to his left showed signs of disturbance and still echoed with curses, and although the man in the grey robe was completely lost from sight Alan had no doubt that he had gone that way. He hesitated, and then remembered Cathy.

He was struck by the sudden fear that the man he had pursued might have had an accomplice, and the realisation that he had left Cathy alone. He badly wanted to continue the chase, but the fast swelling concern for the girl stopped him. He still believed that it was Cathy whom the unknown enemy were trying to silence, and he turned and hurried back the way he had come.

He was besieged on all sides by irate shopkeepers and customers as he retraced his steps, all of them jabbering furiously in Arabic, waving their arms and thrusting out open palms for reimbursement. He ignored them all and strode forcefully through the crush with a steadily mounting anxiety in his heart. He should have known that he could not catch a fleeing Arab here in his own ground of the medina. He should never have left Cathy.

He felt a definite rush of relief when he finally saw the bright flash of her orange-coloured blouse through the barrier of black, brown and grey robes that thronged ahead of him. He quickened his pace and a few seconds later her hurrying shoulders were gripped beneath his steadying hands. Her face was pale and her mouth trembled a little. The flecked, honey-brown eyes stared thankfully into his blue ones.

"Oh, Alan," she seemed to relax immediately under his touch. "I was afraid he might have turned round again with another knife."

"No, he just ran like a scared rabbit," he said reassuringly. "I couldn't catch him."

They faced each other for a moment, almost embarrassed now by the quick surge of their concern for each other. Then Alan said grimly,

"Let's go back to the door and retrieve that knife. We know that that couldn't possibly have been an accident, and the knife will be something to show Haffard."

Cathy nodded and together they returned along the street, still ignoring the gesturing shopkeepers. They turned back into the narrow alleyway and passed through the gloomy arch, and here the following Arabs with their indignantly out-stretched hands finally gave up and went back. They walked the last few yards along the narrow alleyway alone, and then stopped abruptly as they came out facing the solid, recessed doorway where they had stepped aside to avoid the donkey cart.

The knife that had quivered at eye-level between their heads was no longer there.

Alan pushed forward and Cathy kept close by his side. The door was so badly scarred and weather-beaten that it was impossible to swear which of the deep cracks had been made by the point of that slender blade biting home. There was no knife, and nothing to prove that one had ever been thrown.

They stared for a moment and then Cathy said,

"He must have doubled back for it, or else someone else removed it for him while I was running after you." She looked at him helplessly. "So now we have nothing to show Inspector Haffard."

Alan bunched his fists and looked round helplessly. Ten yards away an old Arab was hunched half asleep in a small cubby-hole shop, open to the street and jammed full of dried yellow dates and sacks of grain. Alan strode towards him and shook him awake.

"There was a knife sticking in that

door." He pointed angrily. "Did you see who took it away?"

The man cringed and whined in Arabic.

Alan's temper was suffering. "Did you see the man who threw the knife?" he demanded harshly.

The shopkeeper protested volubly in Arabic and then Cathy repeated the questions in French. The old man protested again.

Cathy said wearily, "He knows nothing. He saw nothing. He was asleep. Whether he saw anything or not he would say exactly the same."

Alan snorted angrily and crossed to an almost identical cubby-hole on the opposite side of the street, except that this one was filled with fly-blown grapes, pomegranates and barbary figs. The ragged owner flinched back apprehensively.

Alan repeated his demands and again Cathy put them into French. Again they received a vigorous headshake and denial. After two more fruitless efforts Alan gave up and realised that nobody was going to admit to seeing anything.

There was nothing to do then but return to the hotel Siroco. The hotel was situated near the edge of the medina and only a stone's throw from the neon-lit Place Mohammed The Fifth, the centre thoroughfare of Casablanca over-looked by the tallest white colossus of be-windowed concrete. It was dusk, and growing cooler, and after a brief meal in the hotel restaurant they both retired to Cathy's room.

It was simply a bedroom with an adjoining bath, and Cathy sat down on the edge of the bed while Alan glanced out of the window into the street below and then drew the slatted blinds. He came back and switched on the light and then pulled a chair up beside her. He said quietly.

"Well, Cathy, that knife that was thrown at us in the medina at least proves one thing. Somebody does want to get you out of the way. The knife was a deliberate attempt to kill you, and that makes it certain that that falling wall in Marrakech was no accident either. And in the circumstances nothing will now convince me that your uncle was not murdered — cleverly and in full view of a whole audience of witnesses, but murdered just the same."

Cathy looked at him and wet her lips, she had been very quiet since the incident in the medina. Now she said,

"We still can't be sure whether it's me or you that they're after, because that knife struck exactly between us, and could just as easily have been intended for your throat as mine, but as you say, we can definitely rule out any possibility of accidents now. My uncle must have been murdered. But knowing it ourselves and proving it to Haffard is not exactly the same. We can't show anything to prove that a knife was thrown at us, and theoretically we're still back where we started this morning."

Alan frowned. "Even so, I'm prepared to go back to Marrakech and tell everything to Haffard. Now that we're certain ourselves I feel confident in insisting that he makes some closer enquiries. He still has that snake-charmer under arrest, and there's a good chance that the man will just break down and clear everything up if Haffard questions him under pressure."

Cathy was dubious. "I don't know. At this stage if Haffard chooses not to believe us then there's practically nothing we can do about it. You said yourself that he wants the case closed, so even if he does believe us he still might refuse to look into it any further."

Alan pursed his lips and rubbed the side of his face in an effort of concentration. "I think that's a bit unfair to Haffard," he said at last. "True he's somewhat smooth, and he's naturally thinking of his job, but he wouldn't try to cover up a murder just to avoid a scandal. He is a policeman after all. What he would be reluctant to do would be to start up a full scale investigation that ultimately proved to be a false alarm. Convince him that your uncle was murdered and he'd be as conscientious as any other policeman."

"But can we convince him on just our word — because that's really all we have."

Alan grimaced. "We should be able to

convince him enough to have a private go at that snake-charmer. That might be enough."

Cathy was still doubtful. "Maybe, but if the snake-man holds out and sticks to his story — what then?"

Alan said firmly, "I think we should go back to Haffard anyway. After this afternoon it's too dangerous for you to continue hunting for a definite motive."

Cathy became stubborn. "I'd rather go on to Meknes and Fez. We can at least talk to el-Zeba, he was the only other man with whom Uncle spent any real amount of time, and there might be something there. The snake-charmer is safe enough in jail and he can wait there another day."

Alan hesitated, worried for her safety, and then he got up and paced slowly about the room. At last he fumbled in his pocket and stopped in front of her. He held a small coin, a Moroccan dirham worth just over a shilling, in his open hand.

"I don't agree with you," he said. "So rather than argue let's settle it in a civilised manner. If it comes down heads we'll go on to el-Zeba — if it's tails we'll go back to Haffard."

Cathy looked up into his face, and then nodded.

"All right, Alan. Spin the coin."

Alan flicked the coin into the air, caught it neatly and slapped it hard on the back of his wrist. When he drew his right hand away Cathy's face relaxed into a brief, almost nervous smile.

The coin faced head upwards.

Alan put the coin back in his pocket and said slowly.

"So tomorrow we go on to Fez, but after two attempts on your life I'm not letting you sleep alone tonight. You can change for bed in the bathroom while I fetch my sleeping bag from my rucksack in my room. If we must go on then I'm spending the night on the floor beneath your window, just in case there's a third attempt."

Cathy raised her eyebrows and the flecked, honey-brown eyes searched his face. Then she nodded obediently.

"All right, Alan, if you think it's best."

* * *

It took Alan a long time to get to sleep. He lay on top of his sleeping bag beneath the window, fully clothed in case it became necessary to spring to his feet in a hurry. He was also acutely conscious of Cathy sleeping soundly in the large bed only a few feet away, and of a fleeting memory of her in her night-dress as she had slipped quickly out of her robe and into her bed. The combination was disturbing and the involuntary quickening of his pulse had nothing to do with the tension of half-expecting to find a hired killer falling on top of him through the window at any moment.

He dozed fitfully, half-sleeping and half-waking, and unable to clear the worried thoughts from his semi-conscious mind. He didn't like the course that Cathy insisted upon taking, and it was strange how after knowing her for no more than a day he should be so concerned for her welfare. He knew that his anger could have killed that knife-thrower this afternoon, if the man

102

had not made good his escape, and he felt that he would have no compunction about maiming or killing anyone who came into this room tonight. And yet previously the nearest he had ever come to violence was a half-hearted fist fight with a schoolboy at the age of eleven. It was strange.

Tiredness gradually drove his thoughts deeper into his sub-conscious, and towards dawn he slept more soundly. The first rays of light began to penetrate the slats of the window blind and isolated sounds of traffic began to rumble distantly through the city. Alan was now fully asleep, but the soft sound of footsteps speared a long expected warning into his numbed mind and suddenly he was springing upwards.

It was only Cathy. It was now fully daylight, and she had slipped silently out of bed to tip-toe towards the bathroom. She gave a little start as he jerked upright, crouching on one knee, and then she relaxed and smiled.

"I'm sorry, Alan. I was just trying to creep into the bathroom to get dressed without waking you. You were so soundly asleep I thought that you must have laid awake last night listening for intruders."

Alan relaxed, but still he couldn't speak. Thinking him asleep she had not bothered to don her robe, and now the bars of light through the window blind were striking clearly through her flimsy night-dress as she stood facing him. She wore nothing beneath the loose folds of transparent silk, and in that moment he felt that there could not possibly be a more desirable body. The sunlight bathed her figure in smooth, classic lines between the blocks of shadow, and it took an effort to wrench his gaze upwards to her face.

She blushed hotly, suddenly realising how much the light revealed. Then in an effort to hide it she said quickly, "I hope I don't look as red as you." And then she turned and dived into the bathroom.

★ ★ ★

Later, as Alan paid their bill and collected his receipt from the desk clerk, the sly young Arab who attended him leered knowingly and said,

"I trust, M'sieur, that you had a most enjoyable night."

Alan realised that the man knew that he had spent the night in Cathy's room, and had to crush down an abruptly furious urge to punch him straight in the teeth.

6

The Prison of Moulay Ismael

Despite their early start it was almost eleven o'clock before Alan parked the Ford Zephyr near the magnificent, ornamental gateway of Bab-el-Mansour in the ancient city of Meknes. The sun was at its zenith and Alan's eyes ached from the long, glaring drive from Casablanca. He closed them for a moment, ignoring the massive splendour of the carved face-work and the arches and columns set in the great twenty foot high walls, and then he turned his head towards Cathy.

"Do you really think it's worth our while to stop off here?" he asked for the second time.

"Well there's no harm in it." Cathy sounded slightly impatient in the blistering heat. "It's only another hour's run to Fez, so we've got plenty of time, and you need a break from driving anyway. Besides, Uncle did spend several days here on his research."

"I know, but if he only spent them in examining the ramparts and browsing in the museum I don't see how that's going to help." He saw the look of exasperation in her eyes, and gave way gracefully. "All right, Cathy, I suppose I will be glad to get out of the car and stretch my legs for a bit, its like an oven in here."

Cathy smiled and they both relaxed as they climbed out into the hot, dusty square. Alan locked the car and then took her arm as they walked through the centre archway of the centuries old gate. Inside was a wide enclosure, a line of horsedrawn carriages awaiting tourists, and above the far ramparts the rising tower of a mosque.

As Cathy had insisted during the drive, the museum, which had once been a palace, was not too far away. They found it easily, but again the curator could only shrug his shoulders sadly. Like his opposite numbers in the museum and library at Casablanca he clearly remembered George Dawson's visits, but there had been nothing unusual about them. Dawson had been interested in the city's history, and the construction of its twenty-five miles of encircling ramparts, bastions and gateways, but nothing else.

They left the museum in disconsolate silence, flinching as they came out into the glaring sun. They walked slowly back towards the car, passing a native wool market where great mounds of raw wool were scattered beneath shading gum trees. Simple scales hung from the tree branches for checking the weight and clusters of Berber tribesmen were busily bartering. Cathy cheered up at the unexpected sight and said,

"Well anyway, we didn't expect a lot from Meknes. Uncle didn't consult any other authorities in the city so we might as well drive on to that old sheikh in Fez. At least we — " She stopped suddenly, glancing over her shoulder and smiling. "Hullo — we seem to have gathered company."

Alan looked round. A barefoot Arab boy of about eleven was trailing behind them, grinning hopefully. There was something familiar about the cheeky face, and then Alan remembered him.

"Oh no, Johnny," he said firmly. "No guide today. You showed me the souks last time, remember." He turned to Cathy and explained. "I passed through here on my way south to Marrakech. Johnny here popped up out of nowhere and became my guide. He cost me about four dirhams more than he was worth."

The boy grinned more widely. "No lady last time. Lady like see souks? Arab souks very good."

"He means the Arab markets." Alan pushed the boy's head playfully. "Not today, Johnny. No time."

"Like see prison of Moulay Ismael," the boy offered cheerfully. "Prison very good."

"I saw it last time, it was just a great big hole in the ground. Now — "

Cathy suddenly gripped his elbow.

"Wait, Alan. Uncle mentioned the prison of Moulay Ismael, there's an entry about it in his notes. Moulay Ismael was a ruler of Meknes around the sixteen hundreds, and he was responsible for a lot of its fortifications. His tomb is somewhere near but Uncle wasn't allowed to visit it because he was a Christian and not a Moslem. He was a bit annoyed about it. But I know he did visit the prison. I recall that he spent several hours talking to the caretaker, he told me about it afterwards."

Alan said dubiously, "The prison is more a series of dungeons under the ground, there's not really much to see."

"Is not far," the boy insisted. "Come see. Come see. This time no pay — no money." Being a natural salesman he was addressing his plea to Cathy, tugging at her arm and gazing up with soulful eyes.

Cathy appealed to Alan. "Uncle did spend some time there — perhaps we could talk to the caretaker. And if it isn't going to cost anything anyway — "

Alan grinned. "Johnny's an old hand. He'll look at us with those same gooey eyes afterwards and he knows damned well that even if I don't want to tip him, you'll make me." He pushed the boy away with a quick ruffle of his wiry hair. "Lead on, Johnny. Let's take another look at the prison of old Moulay whatsisname."

Johnny grinned back and scampered a pace ahead of them, his brown, dust-stained legs skipping swiftly below short ragged trousers. As they followed behind him Cathy gave a half-ashamed feminine smile, and said defensively,

"I suppose I did let him talk us into it. But Uncle did spend some time there and it could prompt an idea — and we are right on the spot."

Alan looked at her sideways and tactfully refrained from answering, but her smile merely became more pronounced.

They left the wool market and the gum trees and crossed over the wide road. The entrance to the dungeons was only fifty yards away across an open space. Alan knew that the open stretch was unfit for building solely because the honeycombed vaults were directly beneath. The entrance was an unimpressive flight of steps leading down to a rickety door that looked as though it might lead to an English coal cellar.

There was no sign of a caretaker, and to Cathy's repeated enquiry in both English and French their diminutive guide simply shrugged and shook his head. He descended the stairs and opened the narrow door, standing aside and revealing only darkness beyond.

Cathy said with slight annoyance, "If we're going to ask about Uncle George then we really want the caretaker."

Alan shrugged. "Perhaps he's below guiding another party of tourists. Let's go and see." He started down the stairs and held his hand out for her.

Cathy hesitated and then took his hand. They followed the boy through the doorway and slowly descended the rest of the steps into the gloom. Alan had seen it before but Cathy glanced around with wonder as they reached the dirt floor. The dungeons were a vast expanse of arched vaults over twenty-feet high, lit only by dusty streaks of sunlight in the occasional places where the earth had fallen down from the roof above. It was of cathedral proportions, silent and sinister, and it was hard to believe that from above there was nothing to be seen but the few crumbling steps and the tiny door.

Alan glanced expectantly at the guide but the boy simply stood to one side to let them pass on. Alan hesitated and Johnny's eyes flinched away in the thin, deeply-shadowed face.

Cathy was already moving forward, drawn towards the largest area of filtered light that broke through a perfectly square hole in the roof.

"There must have been hundreds and hundreds of prisoners down here," she said quietly. "Old Moulay Ismael must have had a whole lot of political enemies. There's no sign of the caretaker, though."

She was right. The huge, silent dungeons were empty. There were no other tourists.

Alan was suddenly uneasy. He moved to join her and then glanced back at the guide. The boy still stood at the foot of the steps, making no attempt to follow them.

Alan remembered his last visit with the same guide. Then Johnny had scampered ahead, chattering and gesturing to earn his expected tip. He had spread-eagled himself against the great supporting arches to show how the wretched prisoners of Moulay Ismael had been chained to the walls. He had been active as a monkey, and irrepressibly cheerful. Now he just stood back watching — as though he were scared.

Alan's fist closed abruptly on Cathy's arm.

"Come on, we've seen enough!"

"But, Alan, we haven't seen anything."

There was no time to explain the sudden, overpowering sense of danger and he simply hustled her back towards the steps.

"We're getting out Cathy. Now!"

But now was suddenly too late. Two vague figures emerged from the blackness behind the flight of worn stone steps and came slowly forward. Both wore dark, Moroccan djellabahs, the one-piece robes reaching the ground and the hoods pulled well forward to shield their faces. One of them was empty-handed, and his palms rested lightly on Johnny's shoulders from behind. The boy twisted in alarm, and then the agitation faded slightly from his face as the man behind him smiled briefly. The man nodded and gave the boy a push that sent him scuttling thankfully up the steps and out into the sunlight, closing the single door behind him.

Alan had never before seen a silenced automatic, but the fat-nosed object that the second man was pointing calmly at his middle could be nothing else.

Alan's arm tightened about Cathy's shoulders, stilling her instinctive shiver of fear, but apart from that neither of them moved.

The two hooded men moved silently towards them across the dirt floor, and then stopped only six feet away. Their faces were just visible in the gloom, dark Arab faces, their eyes cold and unblinking.

Alan said slowly, "Who are you? What do you want?"

The man with the gun answered, his voice soft and caressing.

"Names are not important, Mr. Ross. But if you must affix labels then you may call me Abdullah, and my friend Mohammed. They are both good, old-fashioned Arab names, and completely untraceable. There are so many Abdullahs and Mohammeds in Morocco."

His companion continued, equally softly. "And we want you, Mr. Ross. You are so clearly helping Miss Dawson to retrace her uncle's movements that your next stop after Casablanca obviously had to be here in Meknes. We thought it probable that you would visit these dungeons as the sadly lamented Mr. Dawson once did, but just to be sure we paid the little Arab boy to bring you here. I was waiting beneath the arches of the Bab-el-Mansour gateway when you drew up in the dark-green car, all tourists park in the wide square outside the gateway before entering the walls of the old city, so your point of arrival was quite predictable. I had the boy with me and simply pointed you out as you got out of the car. Then I returned here to wait with — er — Abdullah." He finished speaking and smiled faintly at the man with the gun.

Cathy said sharply, angrily, "But what do you want?"

Abdullah shrugged. "I suppose what we really want to know is — what do you want to know? Why are you making your clumsy enquiries?" He looked past Cathy and his eyes grew colder. "You, Mr. Ross. What did Mr. Dawson tell you before he died in Marrakech?"

Alan stared at him. "Dawson didn't say anything."

Abdullah's cold stare didn't waver. Mohammed said softly,

"You lie, Mr. Ross. It is not healthy to lie. Dawson spoke to you quite clearly in English, which no one there could understand. What did he say?"

Alan said flatly, "What I meant was that Dawson said nothing important. He just said that it was a bloody silly way to die, and that he should have known better."

Abdullah shook his head. "There was more than that. Those words would not provoke your sudden interest in the dead man's niece. They would not have sent you chasing to Casablanca and

117

then Meknes. Dawson's words must have been far more important than you would have us believe."

Cathy stared at him. "You followed us to Casablanca," she accused. "Was it you who threw that knife in the medina?"

Surprise registered faintly on each dark face.

Mohammed repeated slowly, "A knife in the medina?"

They exchanged glances and then Abdullah nodded thoughtfully.

"Kerim — it could only be Kerim."

Alan said sharply. "Who is Kerim?"

Abdullah's teeth flashed in a swift smile, and he waved the silenced barrel of his automatic like a chiding finger.

"Please, Mr. Ross. It is Mohammed and I who have to ask the questions, and we do not have time to digress. You will return promptly to the original subject and tell us exactly what you learned from Dawson."

"I've already told you."

Abdullah sighed.

Mohammed said sadly, "And I thought this was going to be such a clean job."

Cathy flinched, and Alan swallowed hard. They both stepped back, amost involuntarily, and after two steps their backs came into contact with one of the great arches. There was no further retreat.

Abdullah said, "In the old days these dungeons saw much suffering, much torture, and much death. It is a pity that now they have become merely a tourist attraction. I think the spirit of Moulay Ismael must be saddened by the thought, the old tyrant would perhaps be pleased to see fresh blood spilling down these ancient walls." He raised the automatic and went on, "We have no red-hot sword to put out your eyes, or pincers to tear out your eyes, but a bullet wound can be almost as painful. We have lost patience, Mr. Ross, and unless you decide to start talking I shall commence by shooting you through the left arm. Now — tell me again, what were George Dawson's dying words?"

"I've told you. I can't tell you anything else." Alan's words were thick, and sticking in his throat.

"Very well."

Abdullah glanced enquiringly at Mohammed.

Mohammed nodded.

"Wait!" Cathy burst out desperately, her face was pale but somehow she refrained from trembling. "He's telling the truth. My uncle didn't say anything important. It was something else that made us believe he had been murdered. We wanted to find out why."

"So," Abdullah's voice was questioning. "You believe that your uncle was murdered. Why?"

"It was — it was a letter. It's in my handbag."

Mohammed started immediately to reach for the bag, his eyes on her face, but she moved too swiftly. She snapped the bag open, pulling the mouth wide so that he could see inside.

"It's all right — I haven't got a gun or anything."

The two Arabs smiled, Mohammed a little self-consciously. Alan was sweating, watching her with a rush of helpless fear. There was no letter and he sensed that she was about to do something dangerous.

Abdullah said quietly, "The letter, Miss Dawson, please."

Cathy reached into her bag and picked out an old envelope with her own name and an hotel address on it. Alan was suddenly baffled, the two Arabs smiled, and then with a swift movement of her hand Cathy flicked the envelope into Abdullah's face. There was a large twist of paper behind the envelope that burst in the Arab's eyes.

Abdullah yelled and sneezed violently in the same moment, a sweeping blow from Cathy's handbag knocked the gun spinning and simultaneously Mohammed joined his friend in a fit of spluttering and sneezing. Cathy grabbed at Alan's arm and the first sharp tickle from the exploded pepper bag reached his nostrils as they dodged away.

She was dragging blindly at his arm, foiling the first impulse to dive for the gun that Abdullah had dropped. He attempted to twist back but those first few undecided seconds had robbed him of his chance, for Mohammed had fallen instinctively on top of the weapon and was already fumbling his hand around the butt. Abdullah was totally helpless, clawing wretchedly at his eyes as the hot tears flooded down his cheeks and his body still racked with sneezes. But Mohammed had only caught the side effects of the pepper bag and despite streaming eyes he was struggling back to his knees with the gun.

Alan thrust Cathy ahead of him and they sprinted up the steep stone steps to the exit. There was a hissing, plopping sound from behind them and a bullet from the silenced automatic ricocheted off the steps ahead of them. Mohammed fired again, blindly into the gloom, and then they had reached the door.

Alan bundled Cathy through, and then paused for a quick glance downwards as he followed her. Mohammed had reached the foot of the steps and was blinking pitifully in the sudden shaft of light. Alan slammed the door shut and ran to catch Cathy at the top of the steps.

They ran all the way back to the car.

Had they passed a policeman Alan would not have hesitated to have gone back with him to the dungeons, but as is usual when an armed policeman is needed, there were none to be seen. They reached the car panting, and then Alan said:

"Where's the police headquarters in Meknes?"

Cathy gulped breathlessly. "I don't know." She leaned against the car to steady herself, and then added, "Not that it matters. By the time we find a policeman and get back to the dungeons those two crooks will be miles away. Mohammed didn't catch too much of that pepper, it won't take him long to recover and get his friend to safety."

Alan smiled at her. "You scared me in there. How did you come to have pepper in your handbag anyway?"

She smiled back. "A good girl always carries some form of defence. Even in England a girl often carries a pepper bag if she has to walk along a lonely country lane at night, and here in Morocco it seemed a simple and sensible precaution. Uncle was so busy with his research that I quite often had to walk around alone."

He squeezed her shoulder gratefully. "Thank God you're the sensible kind. But now we'd better ask someone the way to police headquarters. These people are playing rough and it's time we had some professional help."

"No, Alan not yet." Cathy's face had taken on a determined look and she gripped both his arms. "We can still go to Fez first as we agreed. I've got the feeling that we're getting near to the truth and I want to see it through. I want to talk to that old sheikh. If we go to the police they'll be hours making up their minds whether or not they believe our story, and that will give Abdullah and Mohammed time to get ahead of us again. If el-Zeba does know anything then those two might frighten him into silence if we don't get there first."

Alan hesitated, but he understood. If it was not for the threat to her safety then nothing would have kept him from following the matter as far as he could before finally turning it over to the police. He was aware that he had not showed up too well in the dungeons, that he should have made an attempt to obtain Abdullah's gun and end the matter there by holding the two Moroccans while Cathy fetched the police. He felt now that he had to redeem himself. He said slowly,

"Let's be sensible about it. I'll drop you off at the police headquarters, and you can explain while I go on to Fez and el-Zeba."

As he expected she shook her head.

They faced each other for a moment and then he smiled.

"All right, Cathy. Let's get back in the car. We'll have to get to Fez before our friends get organised again — but after we've seen el-Zeba we are most definitely going back to tell everything to Inspector Haffard."

7

The Sheikh of the Rif

The road from Meknes was good and
fast, and Alan kept the speedo needle
of the dark-green Zephyr on the eighty
mark for most of the way. In just over
half an hour they were driving down the
wide central avenue of the new French
quarter of neat palm-lined boulevards and
pink-washed buildings that had been built
on to the twin-walled cities of ancient,
imperial Fez. They reached the old city
and then, taking his directions from
Cathy, Alan turned left to follow the
encircling ramparts.

They turned sharp right again as the
medieval walls twisted uphill. The road
was hot and dusty beneath the broiling
sun, and ragged Arabs in skull-caps
or turbans lolled limply in the shade
of the high walls. They passed high,
arched Moorish gateways, with glimpses

of narrow streets beyond. A donkey with heavy, basket-like panniers on its sides was led towards them, and a veiled, hidden woman lowered her eyes as they passed. They approached another monumental gateway and Cathy gave the word to stop.

They left the car, and Alan waved away a couple of would-be guides as they passed through the great arch in the wall. Cathy turned surely, confidently to her left.

"I'm sure I can find it," she said. "Uncle became very friendly with el-Zeba, and twice the old Sheikh invited us into his home for dinner. It's not too far away."

The route twisted and turned through high, close walls, and after a few minutes Alan began to doubt that Cathy's memory was as good as she believed. Then abruptly they came to an arched, iron-grilled gateway leading into a small, walled courtyard, and Cathy stopped.

"This is it. It doesn't look much from the outside, but inside it's pretty sumptuous."

Alan looked for some kind of bell rope, found none, and then tried the gates. They opened and he led Cathy into the courtyard. There were slender columns supporting full width balconies on each side, while behind the columns twists of creeper, bright blossoms with large red and white petals, and sharp spears of sword-bladed cactus pleasantly filled the shadows. Directly ahead was an open door. Alan moved towards it and this time found a silken bell rope. He pulled and fragile chimes echoed through the cool interior.

Almost immediately a servant appeared in a spotless white robe. Alan stood aside and allowed Cathy to do the talking in French. The Moroccan servant listened, smiled politely, and bowed very low before turning away.

"We have to follow him," she said quietly. "The Sheikh is fortunately at home."

Alan allowed her to precede him and then brought up the rear. The servant led them through a narrow hallway, faced with marble mosaics, and then out into a smaller, centre courtyard. Here, completely enclosed, the floor was of the same patterned marble, and golden fish lazed in a small centre pool. They waited as the servant motioned them back, and then the Moroccan went ahead between more slender columns and vanished through an archway. After a few moments he came back and beckoned them on.

Cathy entered first as the servant showed them into a large, cool room on the far side of the courtyard. Here the walls were colourfully draped with bright red and blue carpets, and with silken tapestries with rich gold designs. The floor was softly carpeted, and scattered with silken cushions. The room was designed solely for comfort, and apart from two low divans the only solid piece of furniture was a small table containing a silver coffee tray. It was the kind of interior that Alan might have expected to find in a rich chieftain's desert tent, and the tall upright man who greeted them was a man to fit the room.

Abd-el-Zeba, Sheikh of the Rif, wore

flowing, pure white robes, fastened with a golden belt that supported the heavy silver scabbard of a large-hilted, curved knife. He was bare-headed and his thick hair was still dark. Only the greying, patriarch beard and the weakening, watery blue eyes in his lined face showed his great age.

He greeted Cathy fondly, but gravely, and after her introduction shook hands briefly with Alan. Then he spoke in clear, carefully-pronounced English.

"Will you please be seated — you are welcome as my guests."

They sat side by side on one of the divans, and then the old Sheikh relaxed slowly on the second divan facing them. His servant rushed to adjust his cushions but el-Zeba waved him away. The old Arab seemed to have aged twenty years in the simple act of sitting down, and Alan marvelled at the pride and bearing that had made him stand upright to greet them.

The Sheikh said, "I have read of your uncle's death, child, and I grieve for him. Sometimes the will of Allah is hard, and your uncle was a good man who could humour an old one's whim. Your sorrows are my sorrows."

He paused, and then asked, "But how may I help you, child? What do you wish of one so old?"

Cathy looked faintly embarrassed at being addressed as a child in front of Alan, but she tried to ignore it. They had decided during the drive from Meknes that there was no further point in keeping up their story of continuing Dawson's research at this stage. Abd-el-Zeba could prove more helpful if they were completely frank, and as they were going straight to Haffard when they left him it was not necessary to use any further deceit. She leaned forward and answered the old man honestly.

"Sir, we have reason to believe that my uncle was murdered, and we hoped that you might be able to suggest a reason for his death. He spent so much time in talking with you that I feel you might know more of his intentions in Morocco than I do."

"Murdered!" El-Zeba's exclamation

131

was a sound of disbelief, shock and horror, all inextricably mixed. "But your uncle's death was a tragedy — an accident with a snake-charmer in Marrakech."

Alan said quietly, "I saw that accident, sir. And I'm positive that the snake-charmer knew full well that the viper he handed to Dawson was venomous. Besides, since we started our efforts to find a motive there have been three attempts on our own lives."

The old Sheikh stared at him, and then fixed his deep-set eyes warningly on Cathy.

Cathy explained fully, and without flinching, and when she had finished el-Zeba no longer eyed them so severely. He said at last,

"Your story is very convincing, child — and I cannot for one moment believe that you would lie. But if this is so why have you not told the police? Why, the newspapers say that the affair is closed, and that the snake-charmer has already been released."

"What!" Alan jerked upright.

El-Zeba nodded. "It is true. The man

was released this morning. The Inspector in charge of the matter has decided that any case for manslaughter could only be brought against the missing assistant, whose task it was to milk the snakes of their venom. The snake-charmer has lost his livelihood, for he will not be allowed to perform again, and so it is felt that he has paid for any blame that may be laid at his feet." He paused. "If you wish I will ask my servant to bring the paper. It is written in French."

"No," Cathy said hurriedly. "That isn't necessary. It's just that it's so disappointing. We were hoping that if we can find a motive to help us prove that my uncle was murdered, then we could persuade Inspector Haffard to make the snake-charmer talk. But if the man has already been released — "

The Sheikh frowned. "If you can convince this Inspector Haffard that it is necessary, then I do not doubt that he can find this snake-charmer again. Now tell me, please, why you think that I could help you. To the best of my knowledge your uncle was simply writing a book."

Cathy said helplessly, "To the best of *our* knowledge that was all that he was doing. We can't find anything to suggest that he might have been involved in anything else. And yet we are sure he was murdered, so there must be a motive somewhere." She looked at the old Arab with pleading eyes. "Could you tell us the main topics of your interviews with my uncle — there just might be a clue that would help?"

"I will gladly tell you anything you wish to know, but your uncle enquired only about Morocco. About her people and their customs. And mostly about my people, the Rif tribes of the high Atlas. We spoke too of the Rif war of forty years ago, when my people rose against the French under my friend Abd-el-Krim. In those days we hated everything French, and fought a savage war. Now that time is forgotten but for a handful of dying warriors like myself, who have outlived our natural span."

Alan said slowly, "Dawson spoke to a Frenchman in Casablanca, General Emile Laurand, he too fought in the

Rif wars, and Dawson seemed especially interested."

The old Sheikh smiled. "Yes, Mr. Dawson spoke of the General. And I too have met Emile Laurand. It was some years ago, but even then we were both old enough to remember without malice. We had an interesting talk, and I would like to meet the Frenchman again."

Cathy said hesitantly, "Perhaps you can tell us your side of the story. If my uncle was so interested there might be something there."

"I doubt it," el-Zeba shrugged his thin shoulders. "The Rif insurrection is too far in the past. I was a young man then, a firebrand — a hot-head, as you would say. I was one of the first to lead my people in support of Abd-el-Krim after he sacked the Spanish outpost at Anual. I was with him when he reached the walls of Melilla, and I was one of those who spoke against him when he decided against the massacre of the city. By then I had blooded my sword a dozen times at the Spanish outposts we had found in our path, and to me war was a great and glorious adventure. But later I was to blood my sword again, when I rode in the forefront of the onslaught on the French forts in the Taza corridor. I was wounded in one of those battles, shot in the arm and thigh, but I wore my wounds like badges of honour."

A dim fire flickered in the aged eyes, and el-Zeba shifted forwards on the divan. "We should have won that war," he said fiercely. "We had beaten the Spanish, and captured nearly all of the forts of the French Foreign Legion. And we would have won, if only we had not been betrayed. We tried to persuade the southern sheikhs of the Sahara to bring their warriors to join us in the north. We sent a caravan laden down with gold and silver to buy their support, and had it reached them the concentrated fury of the Moslem world would have swept the French and the Spanish clear of Morocco. But we were betrayed. The caravan never reached our allies in the south. And when the French and Spanish joined forces against the Rif we were beaten back."

The dim flames faded and the old

man's eyes were weak and watery again. "But it was all so long ago," he said. "And now Morocco is an independent country and at peace, so that it hardly seems to matter."

Alan said cautiously, "What happened to the caravan?"

"Who knows but Allah?" The old man spread his hands. "It was led by a young sheikh of the mountain Rif. Perhaps he escaped with the fortune? But more likely he perished with the caravan somewhere in the desert in trying to avoid the known camel tracks? Who can know but Allah?"

El-Zeba sighed sadly and shook his head, then turned to Cathy. "But all this cannot help you, child. It was all so long ago. Your uncle was interested, but only because it was part of the history he wished to learn. So far it has been hidden history, for of the few sheikhs who knew of the existence of the caravan all remained silent in the hope of exacting vengeance on our betrayer. For many years our agents searched for the men of that vanished caravan, and the fact that not one was ever seen again made us certain that all had been claimed by the desert. Now even Abd-el-Krim is dead, and only I remain alive. The story is now only a story, and so I told it to your uncle."

Cathy said tentatively, "Didn't you talk of anything applicable to present-day Morocco?"

El-Zeba smiled. "My child, what would I know of present-day Morocco? I am nearing my rendezvous with Allah. My life is over and I can only dream. The young will tell you more about present-day Morocco, the young who look to the future. I only look to the past." He smiled again. "That I also told your uncle."

There was silence for a moment and then Alan asked, "Did Dawson discuss his future plans? For instance, where he intended to go after leaving Fez?"

"To Marrakech, of course," el-Zeba shrugged. "From there I think he wished to go south, to Zagora and the Sahara. He wanted to see that part of the country, and also to visit the ruins of one of the Foreign Legion blockhouses in the desert.

From there I don't know."

There was another awkward pause, and then the old man said, "I feel that I have not helped you, but there is no more that I can say. What will you do now?"

Cathy looked glum. "Return to Marrakech I suppose, and trust to Inspector Haffard."

"That is wise. I think you should have trusted the policeman before." El-Zeba reached out one gnarled, slightly quivering hand and touched her shoulder. "May Allah the compassionate guide your footsteps."

It was plain that they had tired the old Sheikh, and that the interview was over. Cathy thanked him, insisting that he remained seated, and then the servant appeared, silently on some invisible cue, to show them out.

Once they were back in the street Alan said bitterly,

"Past history, that's all your uncle ever seemed to be interested in. Do you think that there could possibly be a connection somewhere? Or is it more likely that either el-Zeba or Emile Laurand have been lying to us?"

Cathy said shortly, "I don't think either of those old men were lying. And I don't think my uncle's death had any connection with past history. I think that he just stumbled on something by accident, something that even he didn't realise was important. That seems the only answer now."

Alan lacked her absolute faith in Laurand and the Sheikh, but he refrained from argument. He said bluntly,

"In any case, we've reached the end of the trail. From here it only leads back to Marrakech. It's a long drive so we might as well get started, we can practise our story for Haffard on the way."

Cathy nodded moodily, reluctantly, and then abruptly her expression changed and her body sprang to attention.

"Alan — look!"

Alan looked. Directly opposite them was a small Moorish café, a cramped, dingy-looking place with two rickety tables standing by the open door. The café had only one window, and framed in its bottom left-hand corner was a staring, wide-eyed face.

Cathy said shrilly, "It's Achmed!"

The face vanished abruptly, but in the fleeting second that it had been there Alan had also recognised the swarthy, pock-marked features, surmounted by the bright red fez. It was the face of the Arab guide who had prompted George Dawson to his death in the Djemaa el Fina at Marrakech.

8

Dante's Inferno

Alan didn't hesitate as he dived towards the café. Achmed had played a definite part in staging Dawson's murder and his unexpected appearance here in Fez offered a last, desperate chance to uncover some solid evidence to take before Haffard. Cathy yelled anxiously from behind him and he leapt through the open doorway just in time to see the tail ends of the guide's robes disappearing through a back door behind the bar counter.

There were startled yelps from a group of Arabs seated round one of the small tables in the corner, and the fat, greasy-looking proprietor slammed down the counter flap to bar Alan's path. The fat man shouted an angry splutter of Arabic, shaking his head vigorously behind outstretched, restraining arms.

Alan knocked the flap upwards again without checking his stride, allowing it to fall with a shuddering crash on the counter as he brushed the protesting proprietor aside and flung himself into the back environs of the café in pursuit of his quarry.

He was in a cupboard-sized room, stacked with crates of soft drinks and open sacks of green mint, and another stride took him through the far exit into a narrow street that was almost identical to the one he had left. Achmed was twenty yards ahead of him, sprinting through a low arched tunnel. Alan burst into a run again and was dimly aware that Cathy had followed him through the café and was now close behind him.

He ran as he had never run before, knowing that if he allowed Achmed to increase his lead then the guide would instantly vanish in the intricate maze of narrow alleys, and determined not to allow that to happen. He had lost the knife-thrower in the medina of Casablanca by being too slow, and now that chance had given him a second opportunity to come to physical grips with one of their elusive enemies he exerted every effort to get the utmost speed from his sprinting feet.

The fleeing guide headed into the heart of the tangled alleyways in the oldest part of the city, but although he maintained his lead he failed to shake off his pursuer. Alan's chest laboured badly and he was worried by the fact that Cathy's lightly clattering heels had faded behind him, but still he chased his man along the crudely surfaced streets. Achmed suddenly slipped and sprawled headlong and Alan gave a shout of triumph, and in exactly the same second a donkey laden with cordwood logs ambled out of a side opening squarely in his path.

Alan cannoned into the donkey and swore as the beast twisted round, braying in alarm and lashing out one vicious hoof. Fortunately the kick missed its target and ignoring a bellow from the animal's scrawny, but infuriated owner, Alan grabbed at its halter and thrust it back, dodging past its snapping jaws.

Ahead the terrified Achmed was glancing back over his shoulder with popping eyes as he clawed his way to his feet, and despite the donkey Alan would have closed with him in another second. Then the donkey-owner lashed out with the heavy stick he carried for rapping the animal's rump, and caught Alan a hefty clout across the shoulders.

Alan stumbled, yelling with rage and anger. He half turned to face the donkey-man who still brandished his stick and jabbered in righteous indignation, and then he saw Achmed retreating in full flight once more and returned to the chase. The scrawny Arab waved his stick and hurled taunts and threats along the narrow street, and then turned grumbling back to his flinching donkey.

Achmed's lead had increased and Alan flung himself into a lung-brusting spurt to close the gap. They were racing through a more commercial area now, along a street lined with shops and covered over by a bamboo matting that filtered the sunlight through in rippling bars over the robes of the Arabs who stopped to stare, but who made no attempt to interfere with the chase.

Achmed twisted desperately round another corner, and Alan followed him with aching thighs and hammering heart into the quarter of the Carpenters. Here was an even more hopeless maze of huts and blind alleys, each hut containing its own craftsman crouching over a crude wood lathe among a mountain of shavings. There were three diverging entrances ahead and a flicker of vanishing movement in the centre one sent Alan plunging forward. He reached the end and caught another fleeting glimpse of the frantic guide.

Alan stuck to Achmed's heels for a few more minutes of continuous twists and turns, and then abruptly the way was blocked by great red and blue skeins of hanging wool looped over the beams that spanned the street. Alan swore as he recognised the quarter of the dye merchants, and although he ducked and forced his way headlong through the long drying loops he knew that he had finally lost his quarry. It would be impossible to guess which way Achmed had turned now that he was hidden in this garish-coloured jungle.

Alan halted in a clearing among the skeins of wool, which hung like the folds of huge red, yellow, blue and orange fishing nets along the length of each of the four streets leading off from where he stood. His throat felt raw and his chest and lungs strained painfully as he fought to breathe. His legs were ready to buckle under him and he caught hold of one of the loops of wool to hold himself upright.

He knew that he had failed again.

A bare-armed Arab, his forearms dripping with scarlet dye stared from an open doorway in the process of dipping a skein of raw white wool into a steaming vat. The dye looked very much like blood, and the crudely paved streets were running with bright trickles that had dripped from the drying jungle. Alan remembered the description of an Arab guide who had showed him the souk of the dye merchants in Marrakech, and found it suddenly apt. The man with scarlet dripping arms did look like something from Dante's inferno.

For a few moments Alan simply stood there and gasped harshly for breath, and then he moved without hope to ask the watching Arab if he had noticed Achmed pass. As he expected the man answered his panting English with a non-comprehending shrug. Alan swore in exasperation, and then there was the sudden clatter of high heels and Cathy stumbled out of the vivid barrier of hanging wool and collapsed weakly into his arms.

He staggered as he supported her, feeling the thrusting rise and fall of her breasts against his chest as she too fought for breath. Then she made an effort to stand upright and choked weakly.

"I — thought I'd lost you, Alan. I almost caught — caught you when you stopped for the donkey. Then I lost you again." She coughed and smiled at the same time.

He said quickly, "I'd lost Achmed only seconds ago. Ask this fellow here if he saw him pass."

148

She nodded and turned to the dye merchant, a brawny man who had now been joined by two more workers from the depths of his cavernous shop. She cleared her throat and spoke urgently in French. The first man grinned and answered, gesturing down the street to their left.

Alan ducked below the over-hanging wool without waiting for the translation and Cathy quickly followed behind him. The cobbled surface of the street was slippery with dye and once he almost sprawled headlong in his haste. They passed the openings of more shops, and then, after fifty yards, the impeding coils of wool came to an end and the way was blocked by a high wall. The street was a dead end.

Cathy came to a breathless halt by his side and they both stared up at the blank wall.

Alan said bitterly, "I guess those blasted Arabs sent us in the wrong direction. Achmed wouldn't be fool enough to run up a blind alley."

Cathy agreed. "He came from Fez, he

must have known his way about."

They stood panting for a little while longer to regain their breath, and then turned to make their way back. They had to bend low to duck beneath the wool again, and Alan could not help noticing the trickles of red dye once more as they seeped around the large, uneven cobbles. And then suddenly he stopped, staring down at a small splash of red that was much too bright and thick to be dye.

The opening of another dye merchant's shop was only a few feet away, and Alan felt his stomach muscles contract as he saw another vivid red splash in the doorway. He motioned Cathy back and pushed through the intervening loops of red wool, wavering in the doorway as he stared around the gloomy interior.

For a moment the shop appeared to be empty except for the great mounds of raw wool awaiting treatment. The merchants who worked the shop were most probably Moslems attending the nearest mosque for noon-day prayers. Then Alan saw the low, wide vat of red dye just inside the doorway to his left, and the tightened muscles beneath his belt seemed to rush upwards to jam in his throat. In the same moment Cathy screamed beside him.

He turned swiftly, thrusting himself in front of her to block her view. She bit off the scream with a strangling sound as he seized her shoulders and after a moment her eyes opened again and she turned her face to look at him.

She swallowed hard and said, "I'm sorry, Alan. I — "

"It's all right," he said thickly, "I almost screamed myself. Now go back outside."

She hesitated. "I'll be all right now, I promise." She swallowed again. "Is it — ?"

He nodded, "I think it is Achmed."

He pushed her away, out into the street, and then turned back to the limp body that trailed across the dirt floor of the shop with its head and shoulders slumped over the edge of the vat and dangling into the red dye. His face was pale as he realised that although the clothes looked like those of Achmed he would have to turn the body over to be sure.

He clamped his teeth hard together and moved forwards. He knew that if he didn't do the job quickly then his courage would fail him half-way through, and so he grabbed the shoulders firmly and heaved the body clear in one movement. The vat tipped over and a flood of red dye spilled over the dirt floor, and he recoiled with a sudden rush of nausea and let the body drop on its back.

It was undoubtedly Achmed. Even with his face and the upper half of his robes soaked with red the pock-marked features were unmistakable. There was a slim-handled throwing-knife sticking from his chest and the blood and dye were so closely mingled that it was impossible to tell how much was one and how much the other.

There was a retching sound behind him and Alan realised that Cathy had plucked up the courage to return into the shop. She stood with her back to the doorpost and had squeezed her eyes shut again.

He moved to hurry her outside, and

then hesitated. There was something about the knife in Achmed's chest that looked familiar, and clenching his teeth again he forced himself to kneel beside the body. He fumbled in his pocket for a handkerchief, and then wiped the dripping dye away from the knife handle. It looked very similar to the knife that had been hurled at himself and Cathy in the medina at Casablanca, but he couldn't swear that it was the same one.

He reached out tentatively to touch the hilt, trying to steel himself to draw the blade out for a closer look. And then he froze to a sudden yell of alarm from behind him.

A small, wizened old man in soiled trousers and a singlet had stopped dead in the act of crossing the worn threshold. The stains on his veined arms and clothes marked him as one of the dye workers, and his yell of terror and the staring look in his incredibly widened eyes left no doubt as to his conclusions as he saw Alan crouching over the corpse with one hand actually touching the knife hilt. For a moment he could only stare, and then his wide open mouth worked into another shriek and he turned and fled.

The second shriek was a spur that jabbed Alan back to life and he sprang to his feet in panic. He knew he was in a tight situation and that he could never explain his position if the old man returned with a flock of avenging Arabs. And even though Cathy's French might be understood it was doubtful whether anyone would listen to them in the circumstances, especially as his hands were still wet with dye and blood where he had turned the body over. His only hope was to get out before the old man returned with a mob.

He grabbed Cathy's shoulder and together they hurried out of the shop and ran back through the wool jungle. They reached the clearing where the four streets joined just in time to see the old man jabbering frantically in the entrance to the shop where they had previously asked the way. The brawny proprietor of the shop gave an excited yell as he saw them pass over the old man's shoulder, but before he and his companions could give chase Alan and Cathy had plunged into the opposite wool-curtained street.

Shouts of pursuit sounded behind them and Alan prayed that they did not find themselves in any blind alley as the luckless Achmed had done. By taking flight he had now made his position seem as black and guilt-ridden as it could possibly be, and he had a terrible fear that if he and Cathy were caught they would probably be lynched — or whatever the Arabs used as an alternative.

They came out of the vividly-draped coils of the dye market and plunged down a street of cluttered shops. There were now half a dozen of the dye workers behind them, shouting and gathering recruits as they came. The positions were now reversed with a vengeance, and after their hectic, strength-sapping chase after Achmed, Alan knew that he and Cathy hadn't a hope of staying ahead. Already she was beginning to stumble and flag beside him.

Then fate blessed him with another complete reversal of the incident that had aided Achmed's escape. The streets of Fez in this quarter were far too narrow to admit any kind of transport except for the frequent donkeys, and now another shuffling beast of burden jogged out of a side street as they passed.

They dodged in front of the startled animal's nose, diving into a narrow opening with high walls on either side, and acting on the impulse of a sudden idea Alan released his grip on Cathy's arm and turned back. The donkey's head was bowed beneath a load of six foot poles, the ends of which extended well beyond its neck and rump, and Alan flung his arms around its load and its middle and wrenched it completely round with all his strength. The sudden attack would have thrown the terrified animal off its feet but for the poles on its back which jammed solidly across the entrance to the street. Leaving the donkey braying helplessly and their pursuers cursing lustily as they struggled to release the strongly kicking barrier, Alan again grabbed Cathy's arm and continued their flight.

He took the precaution of making another dozen twists and turns before feeling satisfied that they were well clear of the mob, and then slowed down to a walk. Both he and Cathy were temporarily exhausted and they supported each other as they kept moving in stumbling silence, neither daring to suggest that they stopped to rest. They were hopelessly lost in the medina, but by maintaining as near as possible a straight line Alan knew that they must eventually strike the completely encircling walls, and from there they should be able to find their way back to the car.

At length they did reach the inside of the massive ramparts, and after following the wall to their left they passed through an arched gateway that brought them outside the wall again. He recognised the road running parallel to the wall and knew that the Ford Zephyr must be at the next gateway to their left.

As they walked towards it Cathy found the energy to speak and asked,

"What do we do now, Alan? And who killed Achmed?"

Alan said grimly, "I've no idea who

157

killed him. Someone must have seen us chase after him — someone who knew that he would head for the dye market, it's a good place to shake off anyone behind you and Achmed probably had friends there. That someone cut ahead of us to make sure that I didn't catch Achmed and make him talk."

He stopped, still breathless, and Cathy said again,

"But what do we do now?"

Alans face retained its grim expression. "We go back to el-Zeba," he said. "You said that your uncle hired Achmed here in Fez, and now we know that he came back here after arranging things with that snakecharmer in Marrakech, possibly to report to whoever was really paying him his money. And when we saw him we were only a few yards away from el-Zeba's home. I think that old Sheikh might be able to answer some more questions."

Cathy looked uncertain, but she didn't argue. They passed their car and re-entered the old city through the great gateway, and again she guided him to the home of the Rif chieftain. Their breathing was almost normal now, but Alan's face was still grim and determined.

They approached more slowly as they covered the last hundred yards, and then they turned the last corner and received another unpleasant shock. Instead of an empty street there were a crowd of peering Arabs clustered outside the arched entrance to the courtyard of el-Zeba's home, and there were two armed Moroccan policemen keeping them in order.

Alan pulled Cathy back into the street behind them and said slowly, "What the hell's going on there?"

"I don't know." Cathy was worried and it showed in her eyes. She hesitated and then said, "You'd better stay back for a minute, Alan, and I'll see if I can find out. It might be as well if we're not seen together."

He held her arms. "You stay here. I'll go."

She gave him a frank look. "How much French can you understand?"

He realised that she was right and

reluctantly released her.

She smiled and turned into the street. The crowd by el-Zeba's gateway were still too preoccupied with craning their heads to see inside the courtyard to take any notice of her, but she didn't make the mistake of approaching them. Instead she stopped by a small fruit shop barely half-way towards them and began turning over the pomegranates on show. The gawping proprietor who had been watching the proceedings further down the street turned reluctantly towards her.

After a few moments she returned with a bag of pomegranates in her hand and the moment she rounded the corner out of the shopkeeper's sight she ran blindly forward into Alan's arms. He caught her and saw the tears in her eyes. She said wretchedly,

"Alan, el-Zeba wasn't behind all this. He's dead. The police are in there now. The shopman told me without waiting for me to ask."

Alan stared at her, unbelieving. "El-Zeba dead. He can't be!"

"But he is. And that's not the worst.

The police are looking for an English couple who were with him immediately before the servant discovered his body. That's us, Alan. The police are hunting us for el-Zeba's murder!"

9

Escape From Fez

They hurried straight back to the car and experienced a sensation of relief when they reached it unchallenged, as though the car itself offered some lasting refuge from the chain of circumstance tightening around them. They tumbled into the front seat of the dark-green Zephyr, Cathy still clutching her unwanted purchase of pomegranates, and for a few moments they simply sat in shaken silence to regain their breath.

It was getting dusk now, the burning heat had reduced to bearable proportions and the great walls threw a long shadow that completely enveloped the parked car. Cathy was still trembling a little, and she smoothed her skirt and fingered the front of her orange-coloured blouse with self-conscious hands. A wave of her dark hair had fallen out of place but she hadn't noticed. After a moment she looked at Alan with troubled eyes.

He said dully, "It seems that I was wrong. El-Zeba wasn't behind it after all."

"But why should anyone want to kill him?"

"Why should anyone want to kill your uncle?" he countered helplessly. "And why should they want to kill Achmed? All three must have known too much. Whoever saw us chase after Achmed must also have realised that we had been talking to the Sheikh."

She looked at him and swallowed. "That means there must have been two of them — one to deal with el-Zeba, the other to head off Achmed."

Alan nodded. "That's what I think. Abdullah and Mohammed must have got organised far quicker than I expected. I don't see who else it could have been."

Cathy shuddered. "So what do we do now. We can hardly go to the police as we intended now that we're being hunted for two murders. If it was just one killing we might convince them, but not two, especially after that man in the dye market saw you kneeling over Achmed with your hand actually touching the knife, he thought you had only just stabbed him."

"I know. I know." Alan's nerves were frayed and he knew he was making a poor job of hiding the fact. "We should have gone to the police long ago, and now we really have left it too late. They'll never believe a word of our story. With only our own word to back it up it would have been a tough job to get Haffard, or anyone else to accept it even in normal circumstances, now it will be impossible."

She said in a low voice, "I'm sorry, Alan — sorry that I insisted we come here after Casablanca and Meknes. You were right in wanting to go to the police then. It's all my stubborn fault."

His face softened and his hand fastened on her arm. "Don't start that, Cathy, it's as much my fault as yours. I wanted to come here after Meknes, remember. I just didn't want you heading into any more danger."

She forced a faint smile. "It's still mostly my fault, and we both know it. If I hadn't insisted on following my uncle's trail that old man might still be alive."

"Stop that!" His voice was hard and firm. "No one could blame you — not even el-Zeba."

She stared into his vivid blue eyes, eyes that were suddenly commanding and unrelenting, and then slowly she nodded.

"All right, Alan. I'm sorry I started getting weak and womanish again. But what do we do now?"

He relaxed a little, loosening his grip upon her arm, but his face remained grim.

"Well, one thing we can't do is to stay here in Fez," he decided bluntly. "With the police hunting us for murder, and the certainty that Abdullah and Mohammed are also prowling around somewhere and looking for us we've obviously got to get out of the city. And I think we ought to get out now — fast — before the police begin to reason that we might have a car and start putting up road-blocks on all the major exits."

Cathy accepted his reasoning without argument, but asked slowly, "Where can we go?"

He reached out and turned the ignition key, then started up the car.

"There's only one place we can go," he said as the engine purred into life. "And that's back to Marrakech. We'll go back to where the whole thing started — and where we should have started instead of dashing about all over Morocco looking for invisible evidence — and that's with the snake-charmer. El-Zeba told us that he had been released, and that may prove a lucky break for us. If we ask around the medina and hand out a few bribes then we might be able to find him for ourselves without the help of Inspector Haffard. We found nothing to help us in Casablanca and Meknes, and we daren't stay here in Fez, so the snake-man is our only hope."

Cathy was still shocked and subdued by the death of the old Sheikh, and again she accepted his decision without argument, simply nodding her head in acknowledgement.

Alan reversed the car out on to the road and then turned back the way they had come, following the medieval ramparts back into the modern French quarter of the city. He fully expected a siren-screaming police car to pull alongside and force him off the road as he drove back along the palm-lined central avenue, but nothing of the kind happened. The city was busy but serene, as though no news of violence and murder had yet leaked from behind the forbidding walls of the Arab quarters. He drove out of the thriving boulevards and followed the signposts south to Ifrane, Azrou and Marrakech.

He was immensely relieved to get clear of Fez without encountering a road-block, and once on the flat open road he again kept his foot well down on the accelerator. It was dark now and he had switched on his headlights as they left the city. The bright swathe showed up glimpses of irrigated maize fields and stretches of bright red earth on either side of the road. Somewhere ahead, hidden by darkness, were the foothills of the Middle Atlas, and three hundred miles away was Marrakech.

After ten minutes of driving Cathy said,

"I'll switch the radio on, we might pick up a news broadcast." She leaned forward to move the dials on the small car radio, and after turning the waveband picked up a meaningless voice in Arabic. She tried again and eventually picked up some dance music. She left it there a moment and when the announcer spoke in French in between tunes she leaned back in her seat.

"It's a French-speaking station. We might get something eventually."

Alan smiled at her. "I don't suppose it'll be good news, but we might as well know the worst."

He was relieved when she smiled back, and again thanked his lucky stars that she wasn't the hysterical, helpless kind. Providing they both remained level-headed then there was a chance yet that they could extract themselves from the mess in which they had landed.

He was unused to night-driving on strange roads, and although he had become completely confident of his own handling of the Ford Zephyr he prudently reduced speed. Half an hour passed and then they drove through a small town and the road began to climb up into the hills. There were many more twists and turns now that they had left the flat plain and he kept a wary look-out for any unlit donkey carts or stray Arabs shuffling along the side of the road. From time to time the headlights swept over wooded slopes as he took the bends, showing quick glimpses of gnarled olive trees, cedars and bushy oaks, all thriving amid jumbles of pitted grey crags and bright red earth. The hills were fast becoming mountains.

He judged they were less than six miles from Ifrane, the first town on their route, when the French announcer suddenly interrupted the dance music on the car radio. He saw the sudden tenseness of Cathy's face and knew without being told that the announcement concerned the murders in Fez. After a few moments

169

the music returned again and Cathy said urgently,

"Alan, they're looking for the car. That was a special news flash. They know we're driving a large, dark-green, British-made car."

Alan almost swerved the car off the road, then controlled both the wheel and his own agitation and asked harshly,

"How — how could they?"

"I don't know." She thought fast. "I suppose the police must have asked questions around the gateway where we parked. It was the nearest exit through the walls from el-Zeba's home so it would be the obvious thing for them to do. The guides who hang around there hoping for tourists must have remembered us and the car. Now the police want to question us."

Alan said grimly, "Then we'll have to get rid of the car — before we get into Ifrane. Now that that message is out we'll be stopped as soon as we drive into another town."

He slowed the Zephyr down and craned his head forward to search the sides of the road. The terrain was still rocky and well wooded and there was nowhere level enough to drive the car out of sight. So far there had been very little traffic since leaving Fez, but now his agitation increased as he realised that any chance motorist who came past now would be sure to be curious of the way he was crawling along, and would most certainly remember a dark-green British car.

Then, mercifully, there was a gap, a break in the trees where the surface was level enough to risk taking the car. He swung into it and the headlights lit up barriers of low young oak trees and ridges of grey rock on either side. He inched the car forward, afraid of getting it stuck where it would still be in sight of the road, and squeezed it through the tightest possible gap. There was a slight rise ahead and by veering to his left to avoid a tangle of briars he managed to roll the car slowly up to the crest. The wheels stuck and spun for a second, and then the car lurched over the top and ran down into a hollow. He swerved to miss another clump of trees and then turned the car behind them. He was hemmed in on all sides now but he was well clear of the road and confident that the car could not be seen by anyone passing by. He switched off the lights and relaxed in soothing darkness.

After a few moments he became aware that Cathy was looking at him and turned to face her, the outline of her head was only faintly visible. She said slowly.

"What do we do now, Alan — walk?"

He smiled. "Not until tomorrow. We'd best spend tonight here in the car, and then try and hitch our way to Marrakech in the morning." His voice became reluctant and he added, "We'd best split up and make our way there separately. The police are looking for a couple and we can't risk thumbing a lift together on the road."

She nodded in agreement. "It would be too risky, and we can join forces again as soon as we reach Marrakech."

They talked on quietly, reviewing the events of the day and searching for some overlooked clue that might help to solve the mystery behind the murders of George Dawson and Abd-el-Zeba. The heat inside the car began to evaporate now that the engine was switched off, and it became gradually cooler. They drew together instinctively as the night chill became more pronounced, and Alan became more and more conscious of her body beside him. The brief memory of her standing before him in the flimsy, sun-pierced *négligé* in the Casablanca hotel room tormented his thoughts with increasing frequency.

Their shoulders were touching, and a barely noticeable note of huskiness in her voice told him that she too was aware of their intimate closeness in the car. Their conversation faltered slowly, and then they became silent. Then she twisted slightly to face him again. She said hesitantly.

"I suppose — I suppose that if we've got to sleep out here tonight, then I'd better get in the back. We'll have more room to stretch out if we take a seat each."

He tried to see into her eyes, but it was too dark. He said at last,

"Yes, I suppose you'd better."

She still didn't move, but simply sat watching him with a strange kind of expectancy about her. He hesitated in turn, and then the uncertainty flowed out of him, washing away the last chains of restraint. His arm moved slowly, and then firmly across her shoulders, and she leaned forward to meet his first exploring kiss. After a moment his free arm locked around her waist and her breathing became fierce and irregular. Her slightly parted lips stirred with a response that he had not fully realised was there and a sudden rush of protective desire made him crush her closer in his embrace.

Some moments later they were relaxed, but she still lay in his arms, her head heavy on his shoulder and her mouth brushing the side of his throat as she said huskily.

"I don't want to go in the back of the car, Alan. I want to sleep just like this."

He shifted until they were both comfortable and then stroked the dark softness of her hair. Her hand rested on his chest and the fingers moved in a sleepy caress. He sensed the rounded contour of her breast pressing against him, and the warmth of her hip against his thigh, but her presence was peaceful and infinitely trusting. She sighed, and some minutes later she slept with her lips still lightly touching his throat. He murmured her name and a soft goodnight, and bent his head to kiss her cheek.

An hour later she still slept soundly in his arms, her breathing slow and regular. But Alan was still awake. The edge of the seat was pressing hard into the back of his neck, and he was staring up at the pitch blackness of the car roof. His mouth was hard and determined, and he was thinking of the snake-charmer he prayed he could find in Marrakech.

Alan Ross was not normally a violent man, but he was certain that if he could only find the snake-man, then for Cathy's sake he would somehow force the man to talk.

10

The Shadow of the Koutoubia

They awoke early in the increasing warmth of the morning sunlight streaming through the car windows. Cathy stirred first and her movement aroused Alan, but for the moment they were both reluctant to move further. Outside the car a tangle of bush and branches surrounded them on three sides in a bright curtain of green.

At last Cathy said slowly, "I suppose we'd better get up."

She straightened herself as she spoke and smiled at him warmly. Her hands moved self-consciously to tidy her hair. Alan watched her for a moment, and then stretched cramped limbs and straightened up beside her.

They were both exceedingly hungry, for the events of the previous day had moved so fast that they had not eaten since breakfast in the Casablanca hotel, so their first thought was for food. There were several slabs of chocolate in the car, and the bag of pomegranates which Cathy had been forced to buy in Fez, and they made do with those. When they had finished Cathy said,

"We'd best get started before it gets too hot. Hitch-hiking won't be fun at midday."

Alan smiled. "I found that out before I met you." He studied her for a moment, unwilling to let her go alone but knowing that there was no real choice. Together on the road they would soon be picked up by the police. Finally he said,

"I think you'd better change before you start out. El-Zeba's servant is sure to have given our descriptions to the police and that orange blouse stands out like a burst of flame. If you've got some jeans and a sweater in your luggage that would be ideal."

She nodded. "I'll do that."

"Good. I'll pack a few things we might need in my ruck-sack and you can take that and my sleeping bag. If you've got those you'll look the part, and providing you speak nothing but French there's no reason why anyone should realise that you're English. You shouldn't have any trouble at all."

"I think my French is good enough to pass off, but — " She looked at him hesitantly. "What about you? If I take the rucksack you'll have nothing that will make you look like a genuine hitch-hiker on holiday. And you don't speak anything but English."

He grinned reassuringly. "I'll manage. I'll jump the back of a lorry instead of making myself obvious by thumbing. I'll be all right, it's only you I'm worried about."

"Then don't worry." She smiled at him. "Nothing can happen to me."

They faced each other for a moment, and then at last he reached for the door handle.

"I'll get your suitcase out of the boot," he said. "And then I'll take a walk down to the road while you change. I want to be sure that nobody on the road can see the car."

Five minutes later he was satisfied that

the car was completely hidden from any casual gaze. He dawdled on the side of the road for a while to give her plenty of time, and then made his way back to the car. The dark-green bodywork blended so neatly with the background that any passer-by would have to walk right up to it before it became noticeable. Cathy stood by the open boot, now wearing dark jeans and a white blouse as she restowed her suitcase. She closed the boot and turned to face him as he came up.

"The sweater's in the front of the car," she said. "It's a large beatniky one so it'll help the general image."

Alan nodded approvingly and then dragged his rucksack from the back seat. He emptied his own belongings out and together they repacked it with a few brief necessities, including a torch and road maps from the front of the car, then Alan strapped his sleeping bag on top of it and they were ready to go on.

Cathy hesitated before donning her sweater, and asked,

"Where shall we meet?"

He thought for a moment then answered.

"By the Koutoubia mosque. It's the most prominent landmark in Marrakech, right opposite the Djemaa el Fina."

"All right, at least we can't fail to find it." She smiled briefly, confidently. "I'll meet you on the shady side, whatever time of day it is."

They stood in vague embarrassment for a moment, and then she turned to pull on the large, fluffy blue sweater she had laid to one side. Alan helped her to adjust the straps of the rucksack across her shoulders and then walked with her to the road.

"I'll give you an hour or so to get well ahead," he said quietly. "And then I'll follow."

They hesitated uncertainly, and then parted. Cathy's shoulders were upright, unaffected by the light load, and she walked firmly with a confidence that she didn't quite feel. Alan watched her moving off down the road. She looked back once before passing round the first corner, and then he went back to the car.

He spent the next hour in loitering

impatiently near the car, and glancing frequently at his watch. He was well clear of the road, but still close enough to hear the occasional car or lorry go past, and at the end of the hour he judged that Cathy should have got a lift and be well on her way by now. It was time to begin his own journey.

He went back into the car to select a clean brown shirt from his clothes on the back seat, which was the best he could do to changing his description from the one that had undoubtedly been circulated by the police. Then he carefully locked all the car doors and the boot. He walked back to the road and began walking briskly towards Ifrane.

The sun was already uncomfortably hot, and promising another gruelling day. The scenery was ruggedly attractive with oaks, olives, boulders and splashes of red earth all shaken aimlessly together. There were glimpses of the beginnings of cedar forests high to the left, while on his right the mountain slopes fell steeply and he could see vast sweeps of red, semi-desert plains through the tops of the trees.

Traffic was slight but each time he heard the sound of an approaching engine he played safe and scrambled out of sight until it was past.

He walked several miles before he ultimately found the kind of spot he was looking for; a cleared space off the right-hand side of the road with criss-crossed tyre marks and a litter of discarded papers and cigarette packets clearly marked as a lay-by. He studied it for a moment, and then found a concealed spot behind a bush-strangled outcrop of granite rocks and settled down to wait.

After ten minutes a large lorry pulled in, but it was heading in the wrong direction and after the first reaction of tightening muscles Alan relaxed again to watch. Two Moroccans in drab blue overalls swung out of the cab, stretching and then leaning against the bonnet. One of them yawned and the other produced cigarettes. They smoked slowly and then the yawning one climbed back into the cab, returning with two bottles of Coco-Cola and two long French loaves, split and filled up the middle. They sat side by side on the lorry's fender and began a late breakfast.

The two men were in no hurry, and were still finishing the last of the coke bottles fifteen minutes later when a second lorry pulled in. The new arrival was simply a cab and long trailer carrying a load of timber, but it was headed south towards Marrakech. The driver and his mate exchanged grinning greetings with the crew of the first lorry.

Alan tensed, for this was what he had been waiting for, but for the moment he could not reach the back of the timber trailer without being spotted by the two men lingering over the last of their breakfast. The crew of the timber lorry elected to eat in their cab, which was the best for which Alan could hope, but the original pair showed no signs of moving on.

Alan waited in exasperation, his patience fraying more with each dragging minute. The two Moroccans lit fresh cigarettes and proceeded to smoke them in blissful ignorance as though time was the least important thing in the world.

Another fifteen minutes passed and finally the two men stood up. Alan frantically willed them to go but still they conversed idly for several more moments before returning to their cab. Alan breathed a sigh of relief as the driver leaned forward and the engine roared, and then the relief evaporated as the timber lorry started up in the same moment.

Alan cursed with the bitter conviction that even now the timber lorry was going to be the first to pull out, and then slowly the Fez-bound lorry began to move. Alan watched it lurch across the clearing and then out on to the road, but by then the timber lorry was also trundling forward.

He hurled caution aside and jumped to his feet in pursuit, determined that after all this waiting he wasn't going to be left behind. The retreating lorry was already at the edge of the lay-by and he put on a spurt to catch it as it bumped on to the road. The load of timber was lashed into two separate stacks of different-sized planks, both overhanging the tail end, and Alan dived between them just in time to grab the end of the trailer as the lorry gathered speed. He heaved himself up and wriggled forward. The lorry jolted on and he realised thankfully that he was aboard unseen.

He regained his breath and then sat up carefully. The narrow gangway through the trailer's separated load gave him just enough room to twist round and face the road behind him. He was reasonably concealed and provided he lay flat then it was unlikely that he would be noticed until the lorry reached its destination. The only drawback to his position was that there was no escape from the burning sun, the load of timber fenced him in on both sides but there was no protection overhead.

However, there was nothing he could do but make the best of it. He stretched full length and settled himself as comfortably as possible with his arms folded to pillow his chin. He watched the dusty road flashing past from beneath the tail end of the lorry and prepared to endure the journey and the worry of wondering how Cathy was faring.

The lorry passed through the mountain towns of Ifrane and Azrou without stopping, and Alan became hopeful that it would take him all the way to Marrakech. He kept a close watch on the passing roadside but saw no sign of Cathy in her distinctive blue sweater, until finally he felt sure that she must have received a lift and be well ahead of him. By then the powerful North African sun was directly overhead and beating down full upon his back and shoulders. He found a handkerchief in his pocket to spread across his head and the back of his neck but there was nothing else he could do to escape the blazing heat.

Soon his throat was parched and thick with the dust thrown up by passing traffic, his armpits were soaked with sweat and spasms of cramp tortured his body. Marrakech was still over two hundred miles away and he tried to take his mind off his ordeal by returning to the problem of Dawson's, and now el-Zeba's murders. He failed miserably.

The hours passed and slowly the sun

shifted across the glaring blue-white sky to give him some relief. He tried crouching instead of lying flat in an effort to ease his constricted muscles, but after a few moments a car came up behind the lorry and forced him to get down again to avoid being seen. The hard floor beneath him bruised his hips and knees with every jolt, and the jolting was continuous.

The mountain scenery faded as the road descended from the Middle Atlas, and the lorry roared on over hot, barren desertland. Here the empty landscape of flat plains and hills of bright red earth was like the imaginable surface of Mars. There was little or no vegetation except for a few hardy thorn shrubs, and far away to the east was the purple-grey barrier of the mountain range they had left. The few towns were small and spaced wide apart.

The lorry stopped once in one of the dusty, one-storeyed, flat-roofed villages, and stayed there for half an hour, presumably while the driver and his mate enjoyed a meal in an adjoining restaurant. Alan dared not raise his head to find out but kept as low as possible. Several times hurrying Arabs entered his range of vision while crossing the street, but fortunately no one inspected the lorry too closely. Alan was hugely relieved when he heard the driver and his mate return to the cab and they at last got under way again.

He had to endure three more hours of sweating, aching discomfort, flayed by the merciless sun and battered by the floor and walls of his self-chosen prison. The road was arrow-straight, over some of the flattest, emptiest country he had seen, and the only life was an occasional goatherd or a wandering Arab on a donkey.

Then, after a total of more than six gruelling hours, he opened his eyes after a weakening lapse of vigilance and saw lines of palm trees sweeping past on either side. They were all shapes and sizes, from stumpy little date palms to high clusters of fronds on tall, slender trunks forty feet high. He recognised the spreading acres of the great palm grove that flanked two sides of Marrakech and slowly some of his strength restored.

Ten minutes later the lorry was jolting into the outskirts of the French quarter, and Alan pulled himself as close to the tail end as possible in readiness for the first opportunity to jump down. The traffic became heavier and the lorry slowed, but it was still going too fast for him to jump off and he could only grit his teeth and wait.

Then abruptly there was a squeal of brakes and a cursing yell from the driver, and the lorry jerked almost to a stop. Alan was thrown off balance but there was nothing coming up behind them and he swiftly scrambled to his knees again. He dropped over the edge of the trailer as the lorry started up once more and ducked to avoid the swaying ends of over-hanging timber. The lorry pulled away and he stumbled to the kerb and sat down helplessly as his stiff legs buckled under him. A scruffy old man in white rags and a turban, obviously the cause of the lorry's violent stop, moved slowly past towing the inevitable donkey, and gave him a long curious stare.

Alan allowed the old man to get past

and then struggled to his feet, he took a few unsteady steps and then brought his legs under control again and began to walk more firmly along the unpaved sidewalk. He felt weak and dizzy from the ordeal that had been far tougher than he had expected, but after a hundred yards he found an open shop and was able to buy a soft drink that slaked the dust from his hoarse throat and helped to revive him. His head ached from the effects of the sun and his stomach whined with hunger, but he ignored both and pushed on, thinking only of the rendezvous with Cathy.

He walked doggedly towards the centre of the city, no longer conscious of distance or time, until at last he was back on the wide Avenue Mohammed the Fifth that ran straight through the modern quarter to the walls of the old medina. He stopped for a moment to stare at the great guiding tower of the Koutoubia rising above the flat roof-tops, and then continued his steady pace. He had seen no sign of Cathy on the road and he was certain that she must be already there waiting for him.

Half an hour later he entered the crowded Djemaa el Fina square, and paused wearily. It was very late in the day now and the mosque tower threw a huge shadow. Strains of Arab music, drum-beats and jabbering voices filled the square, but Alan had no interest for anything but the mosque. He crossed the square towards it and then halted at the foot of the tower, sudden fear flooding through his heart as he stared searchingly at the base of the walls.

Cathy wasn't there.

He completely circled the mosque with mounting alarm, but when he returned to stand in its shadow she was still nowhere to be seen. He tried to convince himself that somehow he must have missed seeing her on the road, but although he waited anxiously until nightfall she still failed to appear.

11

In the Palm Grove

The excited chatter of the crowds and the insistent haranguing of the performers in the Djemaa el Fina continued in the night, but beneath the Koutoubia where Alan maintained his fretting vigil there was silence. Occasionally a straying Arab passed by, keeping close to the road and staring hard into the dark shadows, as though alarmed by seeing a Christian lingering so close to the forbidden mosque and suspicious of his intentions. None came near.

His concern for Cathy grew, and although he reasoned that he could easily have passed her in Ifrane, Azrou or one of the other smaller towns upon the way something inside him remained unconvinced. He knew from experience how lengthy and frustrating hitch-hiking could be, but he had been so blindly certain that Cathy was ahead of him that his mind refused the obvious answer that she had merely failed to get a lift, and his heart was full of doubt. Cathy was a young and very attractive girl, and he could not believe that the traffic had simply passed her by.

His imagination tortured him with possible explanations. She could have been picked up by the police. She could have been picked up by their enemies, for it was not beyond possibility that Abdullah and Mohammed had travelled the same road, they too had reasons for getting clear of Fez. Or, perhaps worst of all, she could have been assaulted, even raped, by some over-amorous car driver taking advantage of a European girl travelling alone across that desolate country.

There was a movement in the thick shadow close to the mosque walls, and his heart beat slightly faster. Then he saw that it was only an old Arab in long baggy robes and a turban and the flicker of hope faded. The Arab glowered at him with weak eyes, and then slowly sat down where he was almost invisible in the darkness against the wall. Alan realised that he meant to sleep there, and felt very much an intruder.

He glanced at his watch, and was surprised to find that less than three hours had passed since he had arrived at the empty rendezvous. It had seemed like eternity. He couldn't stop the horrible visions of what might have happened to Cathy, and then abruptly he made up his mind. He would give her ten more minutes and then go straight to the police headquarters and Inspector Haffard.

The seconds passed slowly, each one like a drop of blood wrung from an agony of time. But when the ten minutes were up there was still no sign of Cathy.

Alan hesitated another minute, and then turned away from the mosque. With no transport and no knowledge of either French or Arabic he hadn't a hope of finding her on his own, and regardless of the consequence he had no choice but to turn to the police. He doubted that Haffard would believe much of his story, but somehow he had to induce the man to make a search for Cathy. Finding her was the only thing that mattered now.

He recrossed the Djemaa el Fina, thrusting impatiently through the human sea of dark, bearded, alien faces. On the edge of the great square the yellow lights of the lined market stalls and open air soup kitchens flickered like a disorganised procession of encircling candle flames. From here the air was full of strange, spicy smells from coal braziers and great simmering pans of mysterious broth. The square itself was the centre of commerce, trade, entertainment, and even religion where one regal ancient stood before a squatting audience to recite the pages of the Koran. To Alan it was a frustration of endless people shifting into his path and barring his way, and he was glad to get clear of the crowds.

He glanced back once to the great tower of the Koutoubia thrusting high into the star-dusted void of the night sky, and then he turned and hurried on his way. He had delayed too long already and a mounting sense of urgency increased his stride. He was cursing his own stupidity in allowing Cathy to go alone. He should have stayed with her.

He passed through the medina walls and headed back into the modern town along the Avenue Mohammed the Fifth, retracing his steps of only a few hours ago. He was tired, almost weakened, from the effects of the long hard day of uncomfortable travelling, but his pace didn't slacken until at last he stopped in front of the police headquarters.

Here he did hesitate at the steps, his resolution shaken by a moment of uncertainty. If Cathy had been simply delayed by bad luck, the failure to get a lift or some similar explanation, then he would ruin everything by approaching Haffard. His own chances of finding the snake-charmer would be gone, and he would undoubtedly be charged with Achmed's murder and probably with that of el-Zeba. Then he thought again of Cathy, and the possibility that she had fallen into the hands of Abdullah and Mohammed, and his face became grim again. His own position was no longer of any consequence and only Cathy's safety was important.

He started up the steps and then heard a rush of footsteps and a frantic voice shouting his name from behind him. He turned and Cathy ran into his arms. She was utterly breathless, but somehow she forced a gasping smile. Relief rendered him suddenly helpless.

"Cathy! What — ? I was just going — "

"I can guess where you were just going." The words poured out in a rush and she gulped for breath again as she glanced past him up the steps. The doors at the top were open but nobody appeared to have noticed them. She tugged at Alan's arm and said quickly, "Let's get away from here. We can talk elsewhere."

He nodded and they moved back along the street, not stopping until they were well over a hundred yards from the police headquarters. By then she had regained her breath somewhat and he asked,

"How did you manage to appear at the last moment? Another few seconds and I would have been inside telling everything to Haffard. What happened to you? Have you only just arrived?"

She leaned on him weakly. "One at a time, Alan. Please. I've been in Marrakech ever since noon. A fast car picked me up only a few minutes after I'd left you this morning and we drove here non-stop. The driver had a business appointment here at twelve-thirty and he didn't waste a minute. He only stopped for me because he was one of those gossipy types who can't bear to drive any distance without anyone to talk to."

She paused for breath again and then went on, "I'm sorry if I worried you, Alan, but I knew I couldn't expect you for hours so I spent the afternoon searching for that snake-charmer. I thought that if you did arrive before I got back to the Koutoubia then you'd assume that I was still on the road and wait. I meant to be back there before nightfall and I didn't think you'd start to actually worry until then, but I lost my way in the back alleys of the medina, and I've only just found my way out."

He smiled, and gave her arm a gentle

squeeze that revealed only a fraction of the relief that he was still feeling.

"Don't worry about it. You caught me in time and that's all that matters." He noticed that her shoulders were still bowed beneath his rucksack and moved to relieve her of the weight. "You'd better let me carry this."

She smiled gratefully. "It is getting heavy, it slowed me down quite a lot when I was trying to catch you. I knew you'd been waiting by the Koutoubia because I asked an old Arab who was dozing against the wall. I described you, and when he told me the direction you took when you finally hurried away I guessed that you could only be going to the police."

They were silent for a moment, facing each other, then he said, "I don't know about you, but I haven't eaten since yesterday. Let's find somewhere and then you can tell me what you've found out about the snake-charmer afterwards."

He swung the rucksack over one shoulder and took her arm as they headed down the street. They found a French restaurant up the next side turning and selected a table that offered a small amount of privacy behind a bamboo partition. The waiter eyed the dusty state of their clothes with dubious eyes, then moved towards them with the menu.

They were both painfully hungry and were in no mood for any strange local dishes, and consequently they both settled for large grilled steaks. They ate with appetites that made the fastidious waiter flinch and caused him to refill the tiny bread basket three times before they were satisfied. Finally they relaxed over coffee and Alan said,

"Now you can tell me what you found out about the snake-charmer?"

Cathy's air of contentment receded a little and she became serious. The subdued lighting made gold sparks in her flecked eyes as she looked at him.

"I don't think we'll find him," she said slowly. "As far as I can make out he's left Marrakech, most probably to return to the mountains."

Alan scowled. "Damn it. If we can't find him then we really are up a blind alley. How did you find out?"

"By asking around. I approached several of the regular performers in the square. And a lot of the men who always want to be your guide approached me, I asked those too."

Alan said anxiously, "You shouldn't have taken the risks. Apart from the fact that it's dangerous for you to wander alone in the medina, the fact that you've been asking questions might leak back to the police."

She smiled, "The medina is not all that dangerous."

"It is for you — especially after Fez."

Her smile vanished. "Perhaps you're right. But nothing happened and I don't think I made myself obvious enough to alert the police. I didn't ask direct questions, but pretended instead that I wanted to find the snake-man to take some photographs. It's a normal tourist request. The guides were most helpful, they'll answer any questions you ask if they think it means you're going to hire them. Two of them told me that if I had two or three days to stay in Marrakech

201

then there would most certainly be a new snake-charmer to take the old one's place and that then I could take some photographs. I said that I didn't have the time, and offered to pay them to take me to the snake-man. But they just said that it was impossible, that the snake-man had had trouble with the police and been forbidden to perform any more, and that now he had returned to his village somewhere in the Atlas. I spoke to the guides separately in different parts of the medina and got the same answers each time, so I don't think they could have been lying."

"Did you get the name of the mountain village where the snake-man lived?" Alan asked hopefully.

Cathy shook her head. "I did ask the most helpful one, but he just shrugged and said he didn't know except that it was far away. He said that I would most probably be lucky and see a snake-charmer somewhere in Morocco and that I must be patient. After that I felt it was best not to keep pressing the subject in case he realised how important it was to me. I didn't want to make my interest too noticeable."

Alan frowned. "I think that was wise, and I doubt if you would have learned much more anyway. It's beginning to look as though whoever paid the snake-man to kill your uncle has also paid him to skip back into the mountains and vanish." His voice became bitter and he added, "I suppose we should have realised that something like that would happen when we decided to come back here. It's obvious that the unknown enemy don't want the snake-charmer to talk, and that they would want him out of the way as soon as possible." He paused as a sudden chill crept between his shoulder blades. "I wonder if he's still alive?"

Cathy stared. "You don't think — ?"

"Why not?" His voice became harsh. "They killed Achmed. They killed el-Zeba. Why not the snake-charmer?"

She said dubiously, "But we reasoned that it was most probably those two Arabs from Meknes, Abdullah and Mohammed, who killed Achmed and the old Sheikh.

Surely they couldn't have moved about so swiftly?"

"I see no reason why not. But also I don't think that they comprise the whole of our enemies. They gave the impression of being strong-arm men, just paid hands for somebody else."

"But who?"

"I've no idea."

Alan was silent for a moment and then he looked up and said grimly, "Let's get back to the snake-charmer. If he's vanished from Marrakech then either he has been paid to go back to the mountains and stay out of sight — or he's been killed. Either way we can't reach him. So where does that leave us? What's our position now?"

Cathy stirred uncomfortably. "Do you want to go to the police?"

After a moment he shook his head.

"No, I don't want to go to the police. After that blasted Arab in Fez saw me crouching over Achmed with my hand actually on the knife I don't think that anyone will believe that I didn't kill him. And I don't want to sit and rot in a

Moroccan jail while whoever killed your uncle and el-Zeba goes free. I want to know who is behind the killings — and why. The only way to get out of this mess is to find the answers for ourselves — or at least enough of the answers to convince the police that we're not making up a pack of lies."

He became silent again, then shrugged helplessly.

"But how? We've followed every possible lead and learned nothing. Where do we turn next?"

Cathy hesitated, "There is one angle we haven't followed." She hesitated again. "It seemed possible when I thought about it this afternoon, but now I'm not so sure."

Alan smiled, and his hand closed over hers on the table, squeezing hard.

"We're desperate," he said. "So let me hear about it."

"All right," she smiled quickly. "It's simply this. We've been acting on the assumption that my uncle was killed because of something he unwittingly learned on his way down to Marrakech, but isn't it equally possible that he was killed not for something he had already found, but for something that he most certainly would find if he had continued the logical lines of his research." She saw the puzzled look on Alan's face and rushed on. "I'm sure that if my uncle had stumbled on some kind of criminal plot then he would have gone straight to the police. He always did co-operate with the police and any other administrative bodies, because that was the only way he could ensure the return co-operation he needed for the success of his books. And his writing was his life. The more I think about it the less I can believe that he would keep any dangerous sort of knowledge to himself. I don't think he had any idea that he was likely to be killed, and if anyone had told him he wouldn't have known why. That's why I think we might have more luck if we follow the route he meant to take after leaving Marrakech instead of searching the route he had already covered."

Alan was dubious. "It is a new angle," he admitted. "But considering that our arrival sparked off the murder of el-Zeba I'm more inclined to think that the answers are back in Fez."

Cathy frowned. "El-Zeba must have been murdered to keep him quiet about something, but what he knew couldn't have been important on its own, otherwise he would have been killed long ago. Whatever el-Zeba knew must have acted as a pointer to uncle's research, steering him towards something their murderers don't want discovered." She looked up, "It's a strong possibility anyway."

"We-e-ll, it sounds plausible." Alan's memory flickered and he became more definite. "Your uncle certainly didn't sound like a man with any reason to believe that his death was murder. Where did he intend to go next?"

"South, over the Atlas to the Sahara." Cathy had the answer instantly ready. "He meant to visit Zagora and the remains of the old Foreign Legion blockhouse in that area. Then he meant to swing north again, heading up to Taza and then on to Mellila on the Mediterranean coast."

Alan thought hard for several moments. "I haven't got any better ideas," he said at last. "We can't do anything here in Marrakech, so we may as well go south to Zagora and see what develops. We can take a bus tomorrow." His voice softened and he finished abruptly. "But if we're on the right track the only way we'll know is if someone tries to eliminate us on the way. I wish there was some way I could get you out of it."

She smiled. "There isn't, and if there was I wouldn't go. He was my uncle and it's my idea anyway." She glanced across at the waiter lounging just out of hearing and added, "Let's get our bill and leave. I'm sure that fellow's scared stiff we're going to run off without paying the moment he turns his back."

★ ★ ★

They were reluctant to book into an hotel for what was left of the night, for they had no idea of how accurately and widely their descriptions had been circulated. Instead they strolled back to the outskirts of the city and moved into the friendly shadows of the great palm grove. All around them the silhouettes of the hanging fronds made black, serrated patterns against the starry vastness of the night sky.

Alan found a secluded spot, soft with grass beneath a stubby palm trunk heavy with unripe dates. Here he unrolled his sleeping bag, which when unzipped opened out like a blanket. He gave it to Cathy and said quietly,

"You should find it comfortable enough. It's a warm night. I'll be sleeping only a few feet away."

She smiled at him, her eyes slightly shining in the star-light.

"It's not that warm and you know it. We'll share the blanket." She sat down on the dry grass and added, "I don't suppose you're any more dangerous beneath a blanket than you are on the front seat of a car, so it's too late to start being coy."

He hesitated and then got down beside her. She lay back while he drew the blanket close around them.

For a moment they gazed up at the stars, and then she turned her face towards him. When they kissed it was long and enduring, and neither wanted to break away.

12

Across the Atlas

Alan awoke as the first pink advance of dawn formed horizontal bars behind the jagged outlines of draped palm fronds. He lay on his back without moving, with Cathy's head cradled on his arm as she lay close beside him. He was warm and comfortable, and reluctant to disturb her, but he had willed himself to wake as early as possible and as soon as there was more pink than grey in the sky he shook her gently. Her smile formed even before she opened her eyes.

"Time to get moving," he said quietly. "The bus services are certain to start early to avoid the heat at midday, and we've still got quite a walk back into town."

She nodded slowly but made no attempt to move. The grey faded completely from the sky and the pink turned to gold, and finally Alan took the initiative and sat up. Cathy watched as he rolled up their sleeping bag and strapped it on to the rucksack and then allowed him to pull her to her feet.

They left the palm grove and began the long walk back to the centre of Marrakech. The sunrise became a burst of flame above the bright green crowns of the palms behind them, and already a few bicycles and donkey carts and an occasional lorry were moving in the dusty streets. It took them three-quarters of an hour to reach the bus station and by then the Arab city was bustling into full life.

They bought their tickets separately, having decided that it was best not to let too many people realise that they were travelling together. There was a small café within sight of the bus station and Alan waited there over a coffee while Cathy went ahead. After a few moments he saw her moving out of the ticket office and she nodded once in his direction. The pre-arranged signal told him that he had plenty of time.

He lingered over his coffee until the ticket office had done enough business to minimise the risk of the clerk connecting him with Cathy, and then he went to purchase his own ticket. The clerk spoke crudely broken English but managed to explain that the bus for Ouarzazate and Zagora would be leaving in twenty minutes. Alan bought his ticket and sat down on his rucksack to wait among a crowd of chattering Moroccans who also appeared to be waiting for the bus. Cathy cautiously faded out of sight, as they had arranged, to get a cup of coffee for herself, choosing a different café.

The bus station filled up with more passengers than it seemed possible that any single bus could hold, all of them clutching great bundles and boxes. The women were heavily veiled and most of them had babies slung squaw-fashion across their backs. Noise and confusion swirled everywhere and Alan was conscious of their eyes regarding him with polite curiosity. He glanced frequently at his watch until the twenty minutes wait was up, and then he saw Cathy return and remain on the far side of the crowd. In the same moment he saw the policeman watching her.

His heart jumped, but there was nothing he could do. The Moroccan constable looked very alert and capable, he was young, his features dark and negroid, and there was a buttoned-down revolver against his right hip. He was staring hard.

Cathy seemed to sense him, for she half turned to meet his eyes. The constable grinned and turned his gaze away.

Alan breathed again. The constable suspected nothing, his interest had been completely unprofessional.

A few moments later the bus rolled out of the garage and the eager crowd swarmed round it as it rolled to a stop. A conductor stood above their heads in the doorway and a dozen rowdy arguments broke out at once. Alan picked up his rucksack and moved closer to the confusion. He saw Cathy moving closer from the other side of the crowd, and then suddenly the watching constable stepped forward and caught her arm.

Alan stopped dead. The constable's words were blotted out by the babble and he was unable to see the man's face. Cathy was facing towards him and her expression was swift alarm. Then she forced a smile and the constable turned and yelled at the crowd, thrusting a passage through them in order to escort her to the bus. Alan watched him hand her up to the grinning conductor and only then did his heart begin to beat again. She turned in the doorway, smiling gratefully, and then allowed the conductor to direct her to a seat beside the window.

The constable stepped back, smiling and then jabbering at the indignant crowd. He stood to one side to let the passengers continue boarding the bus but made no attempt to move any further away. Alan was pressed from behind by a sudden rush of last minute arrivals and was pushed nearer to the doorway. His mouth became dry again as he realised that even now the unsuspecting constable might recognise them if he should realise that Cathy was not alone.

There was no retreat, and he was jostled along until it was his turn to climb on to the bus. He was certain that the constable must be staring at him, but he dared not meet the man's eyes only a few feet away. He pushed past the conductor and headed for the back of the bus, as far away from Cathy as he could get. The conductor stopped him, grinning broadly, and indicating that he should take the seat next to her.

Alan had the feeling that he was being herded into a trap and that there was no way out. If he allowed himself to be seated next to Cathy then the constable's trained mind might link them with the English couple wanted in Fez. But if he tried to ignore the beaming, eagerly nodding Arab conductor then he would make himself even more noticeable. He hesitated, then accepted the offered seat with a brief acknowledgement. He tried not to look at either the constable or Cathy, but he was almost certain that the constable's eyes had narrowed slightly.

He could sense that Cathy was equally tense beside him, and then he felt her move to face him.

"*Bonjour, Monsieur,*" she said calmly,

and then continued to speak in fluent French.

Alan followed her lead, and met her gaze with the right amount of reserve for perfect strangers. He shrugged apologetically.

"I'm sorry, but I don't speak any French."

"*Non parlez-vous Français!*" Cathy played an expression of disappointment, and then she too shrugged.

They fell silent and out of the corner of his eye Alan saw the constable grinning, and no longer showing any sign of suspicion. The last of the passengers were struggling aboard with their precious bundles cuddled close to their chests. The bus was full of noisy bickering and squabbling for seats. The conductor bawled exasperated demands in Arabic and at last the bus began to move. The constable watched it out of sight but Alan dared not pay any further attention to him.

The bus lumbered on through the wider streets of Marrakech, the dusky Berber driver sounding his horn vigorously to clear the way. The heated arguments on the subject of seat distribution persisted all around them but Alan and Cathy sat in relieved silence. The bus passed through the great city walls and then stopped for a final influx of baggage-laden passengers who somehow squeezed into the already over-crowded interior.

There was another chorus of disagreement, and a brief delay while the heavier luggage of the newcomers was strapped on the roof, then the bus lurched forward again and gathered speed. The bickering quietened down into less heated conversations as the squashed passengers settled down for the journey.

Alan glanced at Cathy now that they were well clear of Marrakech and said quietly.

"Thanks for putting on the French girl act. I think it convinced that policeman that we were strangers."

"He scared me," she said with feeling. "When he got hold of my arm I was positive that he was going to arrest me. And even when he didn't it seemed that he must realise that I was scared and

218

begin to suspect. My heart was jumping so fast that I was sure he must be able to hear it."

Alan smiled faintly. "I didn't feel so good when the conductor insisted I sit beside you. I suppose he thought he was doing us a favour even if we were strangers. Probably he hopes I'll drop him a big tip at the end of the ride in return for his help." His smile broadened as he looked at her and he added, "And if we had been strangers his hopes would probably be realised."

She smiled back, and then her expression became serious again as she glanced around the bus.

"Do you think it's wise for us to talk?"

"I don't see why not. It would have been preferable if we could have sat separately, but now that we've been more or less pushed together it's going to look more unnatural if we don't talk. It's going to be a long trip and we're the only two Europeans on the bus and in normal circumstances we'd be expected to strike up a conversation." His smile

219

became a grin and he added, "We're of opposite sexes too, and that's as good a reason as any for two strangers to get together."

She grinned in turn. "I had noticed."

They were silent for a moment and then her face resumed its serious look.

"Perhaps it's as well that the conductor pushed us both into the same seat," she said slowly. "At least it means that we don't have to suffer in silence — and I've got something to show you."

She picked up a newspaper that lay on the seat beside her and opened out the front page. The headlines were in big black print and written in French, but the large photograph of a tall, regal old Arab in full robes was unmistakably Abd-el-Zeba. Alan's body stiffened as he saw it, but he was unable to read the text and turned to Cathy's worried eyes.

"It's today's edition," she explained. "I bought it when I left you sitting in the bus station. There was one of those pavement magazine stalls just down the road."

"What does it say?"

"That el-Zeba was stabbed. He was

found face down on one of those large divans in the room where he received us, and there was a knife wound above the left shoulder blade that thrust down to the heart. The servant found him only five or ten minutes after we left, and the police are still concentrating their search for us."

She hesitated. "But that's not the worst part Alan. The report includes Achmed's death, and the police have realised that it was the same couple, meaning us, who were on the scene in each case. And the knife they removed from Achmed's body fits the wound in el-Zeba's back. Our position is even worse than we realised."

Alan said weakly, "But el-Zeba couldn't have been killed by the same knife. The killer would have had to be in two places at once."

"I know," she said quietly. "So el-Zeba must have been killed with an identical knife. We reasoned that Abdullah and Mohammed must have been responsible for the two murders, and as they worked in a team they undoubtedly drew the tools of their trade from the same source. But it doesn't change the fact that our position looks so much blacker in the circumstances."

Alan said grimly, "Have they identified us yet?"

"No, but they've circulated good descriptions."

He stared at the paper again. "Do the police have any theories to explain the murders? Have they found any connections between Achmed and el-Zeba? Or with your uncle?"

She shook her head. "They've found nothing. No connections of any kind. According to the papers they're completely lost for a solution to either killing. They only know that we were on the spot each time." She folded the paper and put it out of sight, adding quietly, "We'd best not let too many people see we're studying those headlines."

He nodded. "We can't be too careful. And besides, it doesn't tell us anything except that they've damned nigh got enough circumstantial evidence to hang me with — or whatever execution methods they use out here. Our only advantage seems to be that they haven't definitely identified us yet, that might give us a little more time — if only we're using it in the right way."

Cathy grimaced. "I doubt if even that advantage will last long. When they check up on Achmed they're sure to find that my uncle hired him as a guide, and when they get a little further with their enquiries over el-Zeba they'll find that Uncle was one of the old Sheikh's visitors, and then they'll have the missing link that they're looking for. That's when Haffard, or someone else at Marrakech police headquarters will start wondering what happened to you and I. Then the pennies will start to drop."

Alan said bitterly, "And once they can add names to their descriptions it's simply a matter of stopping all tourists for their passports until they get the right ones. If we don't find some answers soon it's going to be too late."

As they talked the bus had crossed the red plains, and now began to climb up into the High Atlas. As they approached the grim aspect of barren ramparts proved to be an illusion of distance and the wild slopes became well wooded as the road twisted upwards. The mountains were a mangled wasteland of green, and of red earth and grey rock, slashed by deep valleys and pierced with thrusting ranges. The bus crawled along throat-catching precipices above vast, dizzy chasms.

The interior of the bus was now a sweltering prison of suffocating heat as the sun neared its full, blistering power. The Arab passengers had become passive and resigned to the discomfort, and to Alan and Cathy it seemed that they were the only ones who really suffered. The Berber driver looked repeatedly over his shoulder and wore his grin like a regulation mask, his forefinger stabbing cheerfully at the horn button on every one of the endless bends.

They crossed the N'Tichka pass at almost ten thousand feet and then the road began to plummet down towards the open wastes of the Sahara. Harsh sunlight ricocheted off red crags as they reached more level road and they passed the first camels they had yet seen in Morocco, a small string of ungainly, high-necked brutes led by a disdainfully bearded tribesman perched on the high swaying back of the leader.

Alan and Cathy continued to rake over the events of the past four days, but the wearying discussion got them nowhere. Neither of them could think of anything new that might help, and in any case it was almost too hot and stifling to think at all. Dawson's notes were still in Alan's rucksack, and although they read them completely through again it was just another wasted effort.

The bus jolted across the desert plains, passing goat herds, donkeys and another string of camels. There were adobe villages clustered round walled Kasbahs where they occasionally stopped to receive or discard passengers. There was dust, the beginning of sand dunes, and scattered palm groves. And then at last there was the town of Ouarzazate, its ramparts and crenellated walls rising like a fortress against the vivid blue glare of the sky.

The bus lurched through the narrow

streets and finally halted in the square. The majority of the passengers began to squabble their way towards the exit but Alan and Cathy remained where they were seated, feeling completely drained by the heat. They knew they had several hours to wait, for the bus that would take them the rest of the way to Zagora would not leave until the present murderous heat of midday had cooled to late afternoon, so there was no hurry. The frantic conductor was again trying to exercise some control over the pushing mob jamming the doorway, and Cathy turned her gaze away wearily to look through her window.

Suddenly she stiffened, and gripped Alan's arm with vice-like fingers that captured his attention immediately.

"Alan! Alan, look — over there!"

He stared through the glass barrier at the pavement where the endless river of veiled and hooded life flowed slowly past. There was an old woman with a child on her back, a young girl with coy, curious eyes, a retreating Arab in a grey djellabah, a Negro, some gossiping Berbers from the desert, but nothing to explain the excitement in her voice.

He started to voice a question and her fingers gripped harder.

"That man in the grey robe," she said urgently. "I saw a glimpse of his face as he passed. It was only for a moment, but I'm almost certain that he's the man who threw that knife at us in Casablanca."

13

Into the Sahara

"Stay here!" Alan rapped the order sharply and sprang to his feet. He dived straight into the milling throng of Arabs barring his way and arguing voices transferred to yells of indignation as he pushed them aside. He reached the door but a thickly shrouded Berber woman laden down with packages and bundles was balancing on the step and holding everybody back as she turned to search for a straying child still somewhere in the back of the bus. Alan made frantic efforts to get past her and instantly aroused the furious enmity of a swarthy, gap-toothed tribesman who was undoubtedly her husband. For a moment it seemed that they were about to come to blows as the conductor yelled desperately above the uproar. Alan struggled against the voices of protest, but no one understood

228

him and he was assailed on all sides by spluttering Arabic. The conductor forced his eel-like body between the two protagonists and made beseeching efforts to keep the peace. The lost child was discovered, reunited with its parents, and the whole family were ushered hopefully off the bus. Alan was still trapped with the jabbering conductor between himself and the doorway.

Alan's temper frayed and he pushed the conductor clean out of the bus, jumping down after him into the dusty square. The conductor howled another protest as he scrambled backwards on his bottom, and the irate family man looked as though he was uncertain whether he should flee or stay to fight off the obviously maddened Englishman's next attack. They both stared in open-mouthed surprise as he ignored them and dashed round the back of the bus.

He was an eternity too late. The street was still full of the flowing robes of shuffling Arabs, some black, some white, some brown, and a dozen other shades. But there was no sign of the grey djellabah and its wearer. The commotion and the delay had given the man enough time to make his escape a dozen times over.

Alan returned wearily to the front of the bus and found Cathy just stepping down. She was talking hesitantly in French to the baffled conductor and was obviously making excuses on his behalf. He took her arm, made placating gestures of apology and regret to all concerned, and then hurried her away as swiftly as possible.

When they were out of sight of the bus she said breathlessly,

"Try not to do anything like that again, Alan. I was sure that horrible looking Arab was getting furious enough to pull out a knife. And the rest of them looked as though they would have lynched you in sympathy."

"I'm sorry," he said. "I should have realised that it would be a wasted effort. If that was our knife-thrower friend he had plenty of time to get away."

"*It was*, Alan. I'm sure it was. I couldn't mistake that face." She hesitated. "What do we do now — is it worth stopping in Ouarzazate to look for him?"

Alan grimaced. "If he has any reason to hide then we'd never find him. But he may not have any reason to hide and he may not have seen us and realised what all that commotion was about, in which case we might find him quite openly sipping mint tea in any café. I think we should find a good restaurant where we can wash and clean up and have a meal, and then just circulate the streets until the bus goes on the slim chance of spotting him."

"You don't think we should stop in Ouarzazate?"

He shook his head. "Your uncle had no intentions of stopping here, he was just passing through on the way to Zagora. I think we should do exactly the same. At least we now know that we're on the right track."

★ ★ ★

Late that afternoon they boarded a fresh bus for Zagora, having searched unsuccessfully for the mysterious knife-thrower from Casablanca. The man had simply been swallowed up by the centuries-old maze of shadowy alleyways and gloomy arches, merging unseen like a jungle creature into its own particular background.

The drive to Zagora took several hours and carried them ever deeper into the Sahara. The road was a ribbon of dust lined with numerous palm groves and more adobe villages with the inevitable walled fortresses of the Kasbahs. The sun was low behind them, throwing long, exciting shadows. When they passed through the Dra valley on the last stretch of their journey the palms made a continuous line along the banks of the river, graceful and peaceful in the darkening sunset. When the bus drove into Zagora it was night.

This time they were the last to leave, waiting until their fellow-passengers had all dismounted. The bus trundled away to its garage and they stood for a moment in the crowded square. Then there was the scurry of bare feet and a grinning

Berber boy was beside them, reaching out for Alan's rucksack with one hand and waving away his slower competitors with the other.

"Hotel, Monsieur? *Good* hotel?"

They hesitated, looking at each other.

Cathy said at last. "This is a lot smaller than Marrakech, I don't think we could walk out of town and find a palm grove without arousing interest. Dare we risk an hotel?"

"I think it's the lesser risk," he answered slowly. "Everybody in the square appears to have noticed our arrival, and we'll have a job to shake this kid anyway. He and his pals will follow us in the hope that we'll lose ourselves and eventually have to turn to them for help. Besides, I don't think the police will be alerted for us this far south. They'll expect us to make for Tangier or Ceuta or somewhere along the coast where we could hope to make our way back to Europe."

"Then we might as well find a bed for a change. And, if one exists, it'll be sheer heaven to have a bath."

233

Alan grinned, and then relinquished his rucksack to their hopeful guide. The boy's face split into a wide-beaming smile and then he was impatiently gesturing them to follow.

The hotel proved to be less than fifty yards away, and had they bothered to look around they could have found it for themselves almost as quickly. Their guide led them inside and stood proudly to one side of the reception desk. A young clerk in a white djellabah appeared hurriedly at the tinkling summons from a small bell on the desk. Alan allowed Cathy to deal with him while he paid off the guide.

By the time he had convinced the Berber boy that they needed no further guiding Cathy had signed the book and the clerk was ready to show them to their rooms. He led them up a narrow flight of stairs and pushed open a door with a gesture of supreme confidence. Inside the room was reasonably large and brightly carpeted. There was an open window leading on to a narrow iron-railed balcony on the far side. It was cool and pleasant, and in the centre stood a massive, Victorian-styled double bed. Alan blinked, and was still staring as the hotel clerk bowed his way out. Then he looked at Cathy.

Her face reddened and she said slowly, "I thought that you would probably insist on sleeping in here for my protection anyway, so it seemed a waste of money to book two rooms. I told the clerk that we were man and wife and booked a double room — but somehow I didn't expect a double bed."

He chuckled softly. "You were right. I wouldn't have allowed you to sleep in here alone. But I've still got my sleeping bag so there's no need to worry."

She hesitated and then moved closer. "You don't have to sleep on the floor. We can share the bed. I can sleep under the sheets and you can sleep on top." She smiled suddenly. "Considering that we've slept together for the last couple of nights we are practically man and wife anyway."

He drew her into his arms and voiced a knowledge that had been with him almost from the beginning.

"We will be man and wife after all this is over. If you've got no objections."

Her lips were infinitely sweet and lingering, her arms, breasts and hips moulding against him with equal certainty. He could feel her heart beating against his chest, the soft warmth of her body quietly enveloping him.

When at last their mouths parted she murmured softly,

"There'll never be any objections."

And then their lips closed again.

★ ★ ★

The next morning Alan lounged on the small balcony outside their window, watching the donkey traffic in the narrow street below. He heard Cathy come out of the bathroom and move around in the bedroom behind him.

"I'm decent," she announced at last. "You can turn round now."

He turned round, smiling.

"You're always decent. Clothes don't make any difference."

"You've been peeping!"

He shook his head. "No, just dreaming." He walked forward and kissed her as though they had woken up in the same bedroom every morning of their lives.

"Your turn for the bathroom," she ordered. "You need a shave."

He rubbed at his chin and realised that she was right. The conversation continued through the bathroom door.

"Let's get back to business," he said. "It's time we discussed our next move."

Cathy sat down on the edge of the bed. "I thought about it while I was getting ready. I think my uncle meant to stay a few days here in Zagora to get the atmosphere of a Sahara town, and he also meant to visit the ruins of that old Legion fort, blockhouse 38 in the desert. I think we should do the same."

Alan grimaced at his soap-covered reflection in the mirror. "Do you think the old blockhouse is really worth a visit?"

"Yes." There was sudden conviction in her tone. "I've been thinking hard this morning, and I've been wondering whether we have been missing the obvious. We know that all Uncle's talks with both Laurand and el-Zeba were centred on the Rif wars and the other tribal revolts of the Foreign Legion days, but we dismissed it all as past history. We've assumed that it all happened so long ago that it couldn't possibly have any bearing on present day events. But we could be wrong. The answers just might tie up with those old wars."

Alan said dubiously. "In what way? Do you think that there's going to be another rebellion now that Morocco is independent and the French have pulled out? A renewal of old tribal feuds perhaps?"

She shook her head. "No, nothing like that. I was thinking of the ruined blockhouse. At the moment I can't see how or why, but I have a feeling that that old Legion fort can provide the answers." She hesitated, and then made an effort to explain. "Can't you see, Alan? You said yesterday that the presence of that man in Ouarzazate means that we must be on the right track in continuing along the route that my uncle intended to take. And so it follows that whatever it was that his murderers feared he would uncover must lie somewhere here, close to Zagora. It's not north towards Taza or Mellila, or anywhere else he intended to visit, because those places are all in the opposite direction. Whatever it is, it must be here in the south. And the only thing here that connects even remotely with all that past history that Uncle found so interesting is blockhouse 38."

Alan came back into the bedroom. "All right, we're only groping blindly anyway so we might as well follow up your hunch. We'll make enquiries at the desk and try to hire a car of some sort for the day, and then drive out to the blockhouse."

He leaned over her, gently rubbing his now clean-shaven chin and looking deep into the expectant, honey-brown eyes. The gold flecks were very pronounced.

"In the meantime, try a smooth kiss," he said. And her head lifted as her lips came to meet him.

The clerk at the reception desk frowned dubiously when Cathy raised the question of hiring a car, his lips pouted and his head wobbled rather than shook from side to side. Cathy insisted that any kind of car would do, they understood that there was no car-hire service in Zagora, but surely someone must own a car of some sort. Alan stood beside her, unable to take part in the discussion which was in French.

At length, after much shrugging, frowning and gesturing, the clerk finally raised his voice in a shout that resulted in the appearance of their youthful guide from the night before. The boy's first expression was a yawn but he killed it promptly as he scented more business. There was a brief conference in Arabic which resulted in the boy nodding and grinning, and eventually the clerk resumed his hesitant French to explain to Cathy. Everybody smiled.

Cathy turned to Alan as they followed the boy out of the hotel and said,

"He's going to lead us to some man who owns an old car. Everything was a bit gabbled but I got the impression that we mustn't expect too much. The man

240

may not want to hire it out."

The Berber boy led them on a zig-zag course through narrow streets and plastered walls, where everything smelled of close-living and passing donkeys. They passed open shops selling strange fruits and vegetables, purple egg plants, red and green peppers, pomegranates, dates and barbary figs. There were a few tumbledown bars serving coffee and mint tea, and open butcher's shops where the raw meat was displayed for the inspection of customers and flies alike. Women shoppers watched them pass with large, sheep-like, endlessly curious eyes. If Alan returned their gaze the eyes were quickly downcast, and there was nothing but the faint lines of brows and lashes above the concealing veils.

After fifteen minutes of twists and turns the boy stopped in the tiny yard of what appeared to be a blacksmith's shop. Piles of wrought-iron work, spikes, chains and camel shoes lay everywhere. There was a ringing sound of a hammer shaping steel from inside a crude shed roofed with corrugated iron, and beside the shed stood an old and very battered Land Rover.

Their guide shouted and the hammering stopped. There was a movement inside the shed and then a man shuffled into the sunlight. He wore a soiled vest and equally grimy trousers that ended in a ragged fringe half-way between his ankles and knees. His big feet were splayed inside badly fitting sandals. He was a thick-set man with heavy shoulders. On his frizzy head he wore a knitted skull cap and his dark face received a pouting expression from a thick brush-like moustache. He wore a cracked leather apron and still held his hammer.

As the Berber boy explained their needs Cathy murmured quietly,

"It seems that this is Arshid, the car owner. And that dubious looking heap of metal over there must be the car." She stopped as the unsavoury Arshid came towards them, beaming brightly as the boy still chattered by his side. He spoke in eager French.

"Oh, hell," Cathy said in exasperation. "He thinks we want to buy the thing outright." She forced a smile on her face and made an effort to explain.

The blacksmith's face dropped as she talked, and there followed another of the meaningless dialogues that Alan was beginning to find irritating. He could only guess at what was being said from the expressions that were exchanged and the tones of the voices, and Arshid's petulant features managed such a vast range of emotions that it was impossible to grasp the trend of the conversation.

At last Cathy turned and said wearily, "His French is atrocious, but he's definitely against allowing us to take his precious car away if we don't want to buy. However, he will take us to where we want to go if we care to hire his services as well as his car."

Alan groaned. "Blast him, we don't want anybody along to give an account of our activities afterwards. Can't you bribe him? Tell him we only want the car for a day."

She shook her head. "He's afraid of losing the car if he doesn't come along. He's very pleasant and apologetic about it and I suppose that to him the condition doesn't sound unreasonable. If we hold out I think he'll only become more suspicious and trust us even less."

"All right," Alan said wearily. "If we must have him then I suppose we must. It doesn't seem as though we're going to find any other transport. Have you told him where we want to go?"

"Not exactly. I told him that we want to visit Mhamid which is the next town south, and that we're simply writing stories for a newspaper. I thought that that would be better than allowing him to draw his own conclusions."

"Good. There'll be plenty of time to ask him about the blockhouse when we're on our way. He needn't know any more than he has to until we've left Zagora."

Cathy nodded and turned to the blacksmith who had watched them with unblinking eyes. She spoke to him slowly to make sure he understood and his dark face glowed into a broad smile. He accepted the two one-thousand dirham notes that she took from her purse with twitching fingers and nodded his head vigorously in agreement.

Cathy said thankfully. "He's willing to start now — as soon as he can start the car."

Alan nodded approval and the man hurriedly returned to his workshop to discard his hammer and apron. The Berber boy from the hotel was grinning broadly again in anticipation of a fat tip now that everything had been settled satisfactorily.

Alan was suddenly not quite so satisfied. Arshid's step had shown a momentary firmness that seemed out of place with his humble attitude, and Alan found himself noting the firm muscles across those thick-set shoulders. Most humble men were small or weak or running to fat, but this Arshid looked to be fit and extremely strong.

The doubts were uneasy in his mind and he began to wonder whether this dubious blacksmith had given way too easily. He seemed almost eager to drive them south now that the first token argument had been settled. The memory came back of the boy guide leading them unsuspecting into the trap in the dungeons of Meknes, and he sensed the possibility of it happening again. Was it possible that the boy from the hotel had been paid to bring them to Arshid? And that Arshid had been paid to offer his services?

He realised that even in the face of these possibilities they still had to go on. And after all, wasn't this what they had hoped for, that the other side would make some move to provide them with a new lead. He glanced at Cathy as Arshid went over to check his battered Land Rover, and felt a sense of responsibility that made his jaws tighten and his heart ache. For the first time he wished that he was armed.

14

The Outpost in the Desert

The road out of Zagora was mostly dirt surface, spearing south through desert and sand dunes. There were still palm trees creating splashes of fresh green and the dunes were a bright red-gold in the sunlight. Behind them the mosques and ramparts of the old town made a centuries-old skyline against the naked blue of the sky.

The Land Rover bumped and rattled as the wheels carved up clouds of dust, but the engine sounded unexpectedly well-serviced. Arshid sat in the driving seat, now wearing a grimy djellabah and a look of rapt concentration as he handled the wheel. Cathy sat in the passenger seat and Alan had jammed himself between them, his knees fitting awkwardly on either side of the gear stick. Every few minutes Arshid would look at them with a quick, blissful smile that was made even more ridiculous by the coating of grey dust that now clung to his moustache.

When they were well clear of Zagora Alan said, "You'd better tell him about the blockhouse now, Cathy. We must be getting close to the turning."

Cathy nodded, and leaned across his knees to speak to Arshid in French.

Arshid listened, his face registering surprise as his dark black-button eyes moved dubiously from her to Alan. When he answered his tone was uncertain. They argued for a moment and Arshid released the wheel to gesture with his hands. The Land Rover veered across the road and Alan had to crush the impulse to lunge forward and grab the wheel. Arshid caught it confidently at the last moment, pulled the Land Rover back to the right hand side, and equally confidently let go again to continue the argument.

Cathy's face bore a look of long suffering patience, and she flinched each time the Land Rover swung across the road. The exasperation in her voice increased as they wrangled.

Alan could refrain from interrupting no longer and demanded almost violently,

"What the hell's the matter now?"

Cathy sighed wearily. "Just plain Arab awkwardness I think. He knows where the blockhouse is, and he admits that he can quite easily take us there. But he insists that there's nothing to see except a few old walls and that he can show us some much better ruins further south, real old Arab ruins. I think that he's trying to be helpful in his own stupid way, but because he can't understand why we want to visit the blockhouse he simply keeps repeating himself in the belief that I haven't properly understood him."

Alan groaned. "Ask him how much he wants to take us to these more magnificent ruins further south, and then offer him the same amount just to take us to the blockhouse. That should settle it."

Cathy nodded and resumed her verbal struggle in French.

Arshid promptly released the wheel again to answer her and Alan closed his eyes helplessly. The fact that the

Land Rover always pulled to the left and their driver could always judge the exact moment to check the swerve was not wholly reassuring. There was always the chance that Arshid would get too excited and leave it too late.

Finally Arshid shrugged, smiling and spreading his hands in a wide gesture of resignation. His hands returned to the wheel again and Alan breathed a sigh of relief as he kept them there.

Cathy said sadly, "I had to compromise. First he'll take us to the blockhouse, and then he'll show us his own guided tour. Like all guides he's convinced that he knows what's best for us, and no doubt assumes that by providing the best he'll earn a bigger tip." She smiled and added. "Once we've seen the blockhouse we'll just have to develop headaches or something as an excuse to go straight back. I'm damned if I'll do any more riding about in this bouncing milk crate than is absolutely necessary."

Alan smiled in return, and Arshid noted the exchange and flashed his own quick, amicable grin as though the brief clash of wills had not happened at all.

They travelled another two miles along the dirt road and then Arshid slowed the Land Rover to a stop opposite a vaguely defined camel track leading off into the sand dunes to their right. The dust-coated moustache wrinkled as he pouted his upper lip and he spoke dubiously.

Cathy looked at Alan. "He's dithering again," she said dully. "He's suddenly decided that he might get bogged down in the sand."

Alan concentrated on the futility of losing his temper and said carefully, "Tell him I'll give him all the help he needs if we have to dig it out and push."

Cathy relayed the information. Arshid looked happier and grinned again. Then he put the gear into first and swung on to the rough track. They bounced along at a maximum twenty miles an hour and soon the road was lost from view behind them. Previously they had passed an occasional goatherd, or heavily-robed Berber tribesman on foot or on donkeys, but now there was nothing but the desert. By leaving the road they had left the known world, exchanging it for a golden expanse of empty, shifting sand.

Alan referred to the Michelin road map he had stuffed in his pocket, it was one of those he had taken from their abandoned Zephyr and on it he had marked the location of Blockhouse 38 from Dawson's notes. The position of the old Legion fort was approximately twenty-three miles south-west along this ancient camel track, and providing that they did not get bogged down in soft sand they should reach it in just over an hour.

The vastness of the desert was in itself frightening, ahead was a million miles of scorching emptiness where only the nomads occasionally ventured, and above the sun ruled a glaring sky where no birds flew. Alan began to understand Arshid's reluctance to bring them out here where a breakdown could spell death.

The track they followed was not much wider than their vehicle, and Alan began to wonder how many thousands of camel hooves had helped to make it in the past? How many laden caravans, rich in gold, silks, ivory and salt, and even human slaves, had travelled south before them? And where had their journey ended? Where did this track continue into the great Sahara? It could be anywhere from the equatorial jungles of Senegal to the age-old trading centre of Timbuctoo.

Alan would have shared his thoughts with Cathy, but the heat was too fierce to leave any incentive for conversation. It was easier to think than to talk. They were both sweating and showing signs of strain, and only Arshid appeared unaffected. The Arab's bad-fitting sandals and huge feet looked clumsy on the foot pedals, but the Land Rover responded smoothly with every gear change. Every few minutes, as though fitted with an automatic timing signal, his face would twist round and flash its childish grin, and then he would stare straight ahead of him. Alan remembered his brief suspicions before leaving Zagora and felt slightly foolish. He was glad he had kept them to himself.

The Land Rover maintained its flickering twenty miles an hour, but from time to time it would skid and slide where the winds had spread patches of softer sand over the hardened track. Ultimately it slithered too far before Arshid could regain control and one rear wheel churned itself deep into the yielding sand beside the track. Arshid shrugged and gave them a look of sorrowful reproach.

They dismounted, their relief at stretching their cramped limbs neutralised by the full strength of the sun blistering at their backs. Alan made Cathy wait in the shade close by the vehicle and then helped Arshid with shovels to clear the wheel. The task took less than ten minutes but by the time they got the Land Rover back on to the solid track Alan was drenched with sweat. He retrieved the strips of matting Arshid had used to give the trapped wheel a grip and then climbed back into his place between the seats. Arshid shrugged again at the natural hazard, and informed him through Cathy that it would probably happen again.

They drove on for another hour, and although on several occasions Arshid's gloomy prophecy was all but realised they managed to stay on the track. The endless red-gold dunes still encircled them on all sides and by staring into the hazy distance they could have imagined that the Land Rover was not moving at all but for the continued jolting.

Alan saw a faint suggestion of green far ahead, and it was so unexpected that he wondered for a moment whether he could be experiencing a mirage. Then Arshid gestured towards it, grinning and shouting to Cathy in French. She turned to Alan with an expression of utmost relief.

"I gather that that's it. The green is a small oasis, and beyond the oasis are the ruins of the fort."

They watched as the splash of green drew nearer, shimmering like a water reflection in the heat. Gradually it split into the shapes of separate palms with lush fronds, and somewhere in the centre of the green was a hint of blue. Then Arshid pointed again and they looked beyond the oasis. Alan stared hard and made out the angular lines of ruined walls.

They passed the oasis, which on closer inspection proved to be much larger than they had first realised, and despite a token protest from Arshid continued a further six hundred yards to the old fort. A section of track split off from the main route and carried them right up to the gateway in the walls. Once no doubt there had been a stout wooden gate to bar the way, but that had long since been pillaged to feed some wandering nomad's fire. The arch above the entrance had also fallen in, but sometime in the past the entrance had been cleared so that it was possible to drive right inside the enclosure. Arshid stopped the Land Rover and switched off the ignition, regarding them with the solemn gaze of one who has done his duty but is not sure why.

Cathy got out slowly and Alan followed her with equal care. He felt rather as though he had been shaken up inside a cement mixer, and was certain that he must be bruised accordingly. Arshid seemed quite content to stay in his cab and simply watch them as they surveyed their surroundings.

Blockhouse 38 had been built in the standard Foreign Legion form of a square, the walls nine feet high and three feet thick and each side a hundred yards long. Once there had been a projecting fifteen foot tower at each corner, but three of these had long since crumbled away and only one was partially standing. The barracks, storehouses, cookhouse and other buildings that had been constructed inside the protecting walls were practically non-existent, mere piles of collapsed rubble covered with drifting sand until even the lines of the foundations were gone. A stone firing platform ran all the way round the inside of the fort behind the crenellated parapets, but much of that too had fallen away. It was almost forty years since a company of the French Foreign Legion had garrisoned this lonely outpost to guard over the camel trail to the Sahara, and only the outer walls had survived the ravages of time and the remorseless advance of the desert.

Alan looked at Cathy and saw traces of disappointment mirrored in her eyes.

There was sweat showing across her temples and she looked suddenly tired and deflated, beaten by the heat. He felt exactly the same.

"I suppose it's no more than we should have expected," she admitted at last. "But somehow I had expected more."

Alan agreed. "Now we know why Arshid thought we were wasting our time. But we might as well have a look round while we are here."

"I'll tell him." She turned to the Land Rover and spoke briefly. Arshid's hands moved in expressive gesture and his shoulders shrugged, he smiled the helpless Arab indication of apology. Cathy turned back to Alan.

"He says there is nothing here that he can show us. There are only the walls. If we wish to walk round them he will sit here and wait."

"I don't blame him," Alan said with feeling. "But we'll take a look round just the same."

They left Arshid sitting in the driving seat with a faintly bewildered expression on his face. His black-button eyes followed them for a moment and then he gave another of his interminable shrugs and settled down to doze. A fly settled on his eyelid and moved slowly down his cheek, but it failed to disturb him.

Alan held Cathy's arm as they picked their way over the sand-blown mounds that had once been buildings constructed by back-breaking labour. Now a few tufts of dry thorn scrub adorned them like dead flowers on an untended grave. They roamed aimlessly, finding nothing, and then approached the ruin of the one standing tower at the junction of the outer walls. They climbed rough stone steps and reached the firing platform that enabled them to stand and gaze through the embrasures at the wide sweep of the desert beyond.

For the moment their own quest was forgotten and the glory of the past and the magic name of the Legion seeped into their imaginations. How many lonely legionaires had paced this platform, straining their eyes across the darkened sand? How much blood had been shed in attacking and defending these walls? For a moment they could almost hear a ghostly call to arms, the bugle echoing through the curtain of time; almost hear the rush of feet and the sound of rifle-fire. It was so very easy to picture the thin line of white kepis behind the parapet, and a stampeding horde spreading like a black, dust-shrouded stain across the desert.

Alan blinked, and pulled at Cathy's arm. Together they moved along the firing platform and into the corner tower. The roof had long since fallen in and the floor was a litter of rubble. Their disappointment was vaguely heightened at finding it empty. They returned again to the harsh sunlight and stared across the enclosure to the far walls. Alan glanced towards the Land Rover and saw that Arshid had now left the driving seat and was reclining in the vehicle's shadow with his mouth open and eyes closed.

Cathy said miserably, "It looks as though my hunch was all wrong, and Arshid is right. There's nothing here. If we were on the right track then the answers must be back in Zagora, or even Ouarzazate."

Alan put his arm round her and tried to smile. "Cheer up, we knew it was only a long shot. We'll walk completely round the walls, both outside and inside, and then we'll go back to Zagora. This damned sun is really beginning to make my head ache, so it should be easy to convince Arshid that we're not fit to take on his personal guided tour."

Cathy shuddered. "The trip back will be bad enough. I couldn't stand any more."

They climbed down from the parapet, Alan leading and still retaining her arm. It was nearing noon and even close by the walls there was no escape from the sun, the hammer blows of heat made every move an effort and they walked slowly. At the next corner, one hundred yards away, one wall of the corner tower still survived to throw a minimum of shade and here they paused gratefully.

Alan wiped the sweat out of his eyes and suggested that she rejoin Arshid while he finished the inspection just to make sure they had missed nothing. But Cathy shook her dark head and they continued along the next stretch of wall. Nothing at all remained of the corner tower at the next junction so it was pointless to stop. They took another dozen steps and then Alan halted abruptly.

Cathy blinked. "What is it?"

Alan said slowly, "It's — it looks like camel dung."

They moved closer and Cathy stared at the ground in front of them. "It's fresh — very fresh." She looked at him. "But we didn't see anyone ride a camel away as we approached."

"We may have missed him if he kept the fort between us." Alan spoke doubtfully, and then added, "Or he may still be around, on the other side of the wall."

A few yards away was a narrow side gateway, and after a moment's hesitation they moved towards it. They were both wary now, remembering their previous brushes with danger and unwilling to believe that whoever owned the camel that had stood inside these walls immediately before they arrived could simply be some chance traveller. Alan glanced at the distant, sleeping Arshid, and decided that he would be more of a liability than a help in the event of trouble.

They reached the side gateway. Through it they could see the bright green of the oasis lower down the slope to their left.

Alan said slowly, "Whoever was here when we approached must have hidden pretty smartly while we were still some way off, and the only logical place he could have hidden a camel is down there in the oasis. I think we'd better take a look."

Cathy nodded, and was close beside him as he stepped through the gateway and outside the fort. They were both looking towards the oasis and took exactly two steps before an unexpected order stopped them in their tracks. Alan wheeled round as his reflexes jumped and Cathy gave a gasping exclamation of alarm as his hand crushed hard on her arm.

Two yards away with his back to the

outside wall stood an exceptionally tall man with brilliant black eyes. He was undoubtedly an Arab but apart from a white burnous fastened by a gold band around his temples, he wore European clothes, an almost military outfit that included riding breeches and long polished boots. In one hand he held a heavy black automatic. He repeated himself calmly.

"I said, don't bother, Mr. Ross. There is no need for you to look in the oasis. I can tell you now that the camel is there."

15

The Secret of Blockhouse 38

For a few moments they simply stared. The tall man's dark face was impassive and even the brilliant eyes showed no discernible emotion. His body was relaxed, and yet somehow conveyed the impression that he would react with effective speed if it should become necessary. Despite the savage noon-day heat that shimmered all around them his face betrayed no sign of perspiration. For a moment Alan wondered whether this could be the mystery knife-thrower from the medina of Casablanca whom Cathy had spotted again in Ouarzazate, but then he realised that this man was far too tall.

Cathy broke the long silence.

"Who are you?"

"I'm the owner of the camel you were about to search for in the oasis.

265

I was unfortunately unaware that the animal had left such a plain sign of his presence."

Alan said bluntly, "That's not exactly a straight answer. What do you want?"

The man smiled, "What is more to the point is what do you want? Blockhouse 38 is hardly a part of the recognised tourist itinerary. I suppose it would be if it were closer to the main road, but genuine tourists don't usually like to travel twenty-three miles out of their way into the desert. Why did you?"

"Maybe we like the desert. What's your excuse?"

The tall man smiled. "Our conversation is going round in circles. It is pointless for us both to insist on asking questions while neither of us are making any answers. This way we only sweat in the sun, and neither of us grows wiser."

"Then break the circle. You can start by answering my last question."

"Perhaps I will eventually. But at the moment I am holding the gun, and theoretically that should give me the privilege of hearing your answers first."

The calm voice sharpened and held the hint of a threat. "Now tell me why you are here?"

Alan hesitated through sheer stubbornness, knowing that even a completely truthful answer would tell the tall man practically nothing; their reasons for being here were so vague even to themselves. The stranger simply waited, watching him with those brilliant black eyes that seemed to drill deep into the back of his mind. He was aware that Cathy's eyes were also watching his face, and that her body was tense with uncertainty and fear.

And then a yawning voice from the narrow gateway electrified them all.

Arshid ambled lazily into view with both hands thrust through the slits in the long flowing night-shirt of his djellabah and presumably buried in the pockets of his trousers beneath. He wore the weary, sighing expression of a man who has succumbed to curiosity but still resents the effort. His approach had been silent over the soft sand and as yet he had not realised the presence of the tall man hidden behind the wall. His remark had a vaguely enquiring note and was addressed to Cathy.

The tall man reacted with the swift, lunging speed that some sixth sense had warned Alan to expect. He instinctively dropped low on one knee, his body swaying sideways in a move that would have avoided any attack as the gun in his hand snapped round to cover the new threat. The stranger's reactions were those of smooth practice, but Alan's were blind necessity. He hurled himself forward before the tall man could bring the gun back again to its original angle.

Alan's chest smashed hard against the tall man's left shoulder, knocking him off balance and spinning him round against the wall. His left hand grabbed at the gun wrist and more by luck than intention slammed it back to hit against the rough-surfaced brickwork where the plaster had fallen away. The tall man yelled with pain as the skin was ripped from the back of his knuckles and the gun was practically catapulted from his hand.

There Alan's luck ended, and it seemed as though he had thrown himself with hopeless violence upon a coil of human steel. The tall man rolled with him and away from him as they squirmed through the sand. The wrist Alan held seemed to twist with a flexible whipping motion and was instantly free, and in the same moment the tall man freed the leg that had been trapped beneath him as he knelt by bridging his body and jack-knifing the leg straight. The right hand with the raw knuckles flipped upwards and descended with fingers stiffened like a falling axe blade. Alan frantically twisted his head and hunched his shoulder to protect his neck and the blow hit him just above the right ear. His body slumped limply on the sand and there was darkness that quivered in vibrations of agony through his head.

The tall man whirled round with fantastic speed, his movements spraying up an encircling curtain of sand. The hand with the skinned knuckles was already reaching for the spot where his automatic had landed but he stopped the movement sharply as he saw that it was no longer there.

Cathy's voice came as a strangled croak.

"Move away from him. Move away from him or by God I'll kill you."

The tall Arab remained half crouching in the sand, staring up past the big automatic into her eyes. Something told him that despite the strangled voice she would carry out her threat, and slowly he moved away. He kept his arms spread wide apart rather than above his head and moved awkwardly until he dared brace his legs and straighten up.

"Further!" Cathy's voice gained strength. "Keep going back and keep your arms the way they are now."

The tall man retreated slowly until they were separated by almost twenty feet, far enough to risk running possibly, but also far enough to give him no possible chance of retrieving his gun. Only then did Cathy look down at Alan and order the still gaping Arshid to look after him. The choke in her voice made the tall man tense, as if he realised that an emotional woman with a gun could prove infinitely more dangerous than any man.

He said levelly, "I hope that Mr. Ross is not hurt. His attack was so completely unexpected that I reacted solely upon impulse. All this is so very unnecessary."

Cathy didn't answer, her gaze kept flickering down to where Arshid knelt awkwardly over Alan in the sand.

Alan was still badly dazed, his head was ringing and somewhere a white-hot spear-point of flame was slowly piercing the shroud of darkness that enveloped him and burning into his eyes. The spear-point became incredibly bright as the outer layers of darkness peeled away and he had to twist his head aside to shield his eyes from the pain. He became aware that someone was helping him to sit up. His head lolled forward and the blinding light left his eyes, but the heat from it burned the back of his neck. He opened his eyes and stared down at his own legs spread apart in the sand, then he looked up and flinched away again as he realised that the spear-point of light was only the blazing North African sun.

Arshid helped him to stand up and the frightened tone of Cathy's voice helped to dispel the last shreds of haziness. He smiled at her and said weakly,

"It's all right, Cathy. I was only stunned."

Cathy moved towards him and he put one arm round her waist and squeezed. She managed a weak smile and for a moment allowed herself to lean thankfully against him.

The tension seemed to ease out of the tall Arab as though he had just been reprieved. His face didn't change but there was an impression of confidence about him once more.

He said, "I'm glad to hear that you're not hurt, Mr. Ross. I admire your courage but your action was completely uncalled for. I believe that we are upon the same side, so the fact that the gun has changed hands becomes irrelevant."

Alan was steadier and his mouth tightened angrily. He looked down at the large black automatic in Cathy's hand and then reached out to take it. She relinquished it willingly and the tall man was too far away to take advantage of the exchange. It was the first time that

Alan had ever handled a gun, in fact it was the first time he had ever seen one at close range, but the solid weight and the deadly feel of it gave him a sense of power and command that became evident in his voice.

"Then why threaten us with the gun?" he asked harshly.

"Merely a precautionary measure. I said that I believe we are on the same side, but I am not absolutely sure. The moment I had satisfied myself upon that point I would naturally have dispensed with the gun. It was merely unfortunate that your friend should choose the wrong moment to wander into the scene. It caused us both to act upon instinct and impulse, you in attacking me, and I in defending myself. I really must apologise for that blow I gave you upon the head."

The gun shifted dangerously in Alan's hand.

"That blow would have broken my neck if it had landed right."

"I am very glad that it didn't. You see, I am now sure that we are upon the same side. I am certain that if we were not then by now you would have shot me, and most probably your driver also to keep him quiet. He has the look of a hired man rather than that of an associate. Perhaps this makes you understand the calibre of our joint enemies, and why I fought so violently when I thought that perhaps you were part of them."

Alan said softly, "All right, let's pretend for the moment that I believe you. If we are on the same side then there's no reason why you shouldn't tell us what you're doing here. What is so important about this old blockhouse?"

The tall man gave him a puzzled stare.

"Then you honestly do not know the secret of blockhouse 38?"

Alan shook his head.

"But I thought that George Dawson spoke to you in the square at Marrakech before he died?"

"He did — but all he said was that it was a bloody silly way to die. He said nothing else."

"Then what brings you and Miss Dawson here?"

Alan shrugged. "Call it a chain of circumstances. We tried to find out who murdered Dawson and why. We went back to Casablanca and then followed the route he took to Marrakech, but we learned nothing except that his murder was somehow connected with Sheikh Abd-el-Zeba who was also murdered shortly after we left him. So we continued the route Dawson intended to take if he had lived, and ultimately it led us here." Alan paused, and then said, "You just mentioned something about the secret of blockhouse 38. It's your turn to provide some answers so I suggest you start there."

"It is a logical place to start, everything begins there." He hesitated. "But possibly you will permit me to move closer, it is awkward to converse when we are twenty feet apart. Also my arms are beginning to ache in this position. I feel like some kind of stupid bird."

Alan said slowly, "Come half-way, and you can rest your hands on the top of your head."

"Thank you." The tall Arab obeyed

carefully, making no hurried movements that could alarm them. Alan glanced aside once to make sure that the nervous Arshid was staying against the wall well out of the way and then he told his prisoner to go on.

"To go on is to go back," the tall man explained. "Back to 1925 when blockhouse 38 was still garrisoned by the French Foreign Legion. And when the Rif tribes under Abd-el-Krim were swarming down from the Atlas mountains to run amok over the whole of northern Morocco. The Rif rebellion was almost successful, and would have been successful had they been able to unite the whole of Morocco to their cause. But they failed. The Rif sheikhs created one of the richest caravans of the twentieth century, the camels laden down with silks, gold, jewels and ivory, and sent it south as a gigantic bribe to induce the southern tribes to join them. But the caravan never arrived."

Cathy said quickly. "El-Zeba spoke of that caravan. Was that why he was killed?"

The tall Arab nodded. "The existence of the caravan was known only to the sheikhs who financed it, and el-Zeba was the only one still alive. But to return to the story. It was believed for forty years that the treasure caravan was either stolen by the young skeikh who commanded it, or, most likely, that it perished in the desert in a sudden sandstorm. But neither of those answers were correct. The young skeikh led his caravan south of the Atlas ranges into the Sahara to avoid the risk of encountering any French patrols. His route swung in a wide loop through the desert and then he turned west again towards the south of Morocco. Unfortunately he was not aware of this deep south outpost of the Foreign Legion, and he passed within a few mile of blockhouse 38."

The tall man moved one hand to gesture over the vast landscape of red rock and yellow dunes that vanished beyond the far horizon.

"Somewhere out there that caravan was surprised and ambushed by a strong patrol of legionaires. The ambush proved to be an almost complete massacre. All but two of the Rif tribesmen were wiped out in a merciless rain of rifle fire, with a French bayonet charge eliminating the wounded. The two Rif who escaped were riding at the tail of the column and managed to wheel their camels swiftly and take flight as the ambush started.

"The legionaires received the most glorious surprise of their lives when they moved closer to inspect the laden camels and found that they had inadvertently stumbled upon a fortune. But there was no time for them to savour their victory. They had been on a scouting patrol when they unexpectedly spotted the caravan, and they knew that there were large forces of hostile tribesmen in the area. The two Rif who had escaped could return at any moment with vastly superior reinforcements. Most of the camels in the caravan had been killed or wounded when the French opened fire so there was no way of bringing the fortune back to the fort. The captain in charge ordered instead that the fortune be buried so that it could be retrieved later."

The tall man stopped and wiped away the first trace of sweat that had appeared beneath the headband of his burnous. It made Alan realise that he too was dripping sweat and that they were all roasting here in the full, relentless heat of the sun. But nothing now would have induced him to interrupt the tall man's story.

He went on, "There was a deep cleft in the rocks less than a quarter of a mile away, and the legionaires unstrapped the saddle bags and panniers from the dead camels and carried them to the cleft. They shovelled sand on top and then did what they could to obliterate their tracks around the burying place. Then the Captain led a fast retreat back to the fort.

"They reached it at sunset and with less than half an hour to spare, for thirty minutes later the reinforcements they feared swept over the rise, and the enraged tribesmen stormed the fort. However, the fort failed to save them, for eventually it was overrun, and this time it was the turn of the Arabs to do the massacring. The tribesmen flowed over the walls by sheer force of numbers and butchered the garrison. Its Commandant led a final suicide bayonet charge in the glorious tradition of the Legion and was cut to pieces with the last of his men."

There was a deep light in the brilliant black eyes, as though despite the calmness of his tone something of the story he told had caused a tingling in his blood. He waited a deliberate moment and then said,

"Only one man survived that massacre. A French sergeant named Soiron. He survived by feigning death beneath the plaster and brickwork of one of the storehouses that had collapsed on top of him. And when the Arabs had gone he walked forty miles in three nights across the desert to the next Legion outpost. Soiron had been with the patrol that had wiped out the treasure caravan, and after a time he began to realise that he was now the only man alive to know its location."

Cathy said, "What about the two Rif who escaped the ambush?"

"They must have died in the attack upon the fort without revealing the nature of the caravan to their allies. It is the only explanation to their silence."

Alan swallowed hard. "Tell us about Soiron?"

The Arab shrugged. "As you would expect, Soiron said nothing about the lost caravan. He hoarded his knowledge in the hope that some day he would be able to return and find the fortune for himself. But he was unlucky, he had four years left to serve in the Legion and before his time was up he lost a leg in another skirmish with the Rif. It ruined his own chances of retrieving the fortune, and there was no one he could trust to help him. His secret remained locked in his brain.

"Soiron, like most men, had strong reasons for joining the Legion, and these reasons prevented his returning to France when he was discharged. He went instead to Cairo, because it was still North Africa. There he eventually bought a cheap café and made his life. He married an Egyptian girl and she bore him one son. In time he gave up hope of returning to

Morocco, but he still would not entrust his secret to any other man."

The tall man smiled. "I can sense your impatience, but here the story comes up to date. A few months ago Soiron's son was accused by the Cairo government of spying for the Americans, he was tried and sentenced to death. Soiron tried to save his son by the only means he possessed — by bartering his forty years old secret. He still had the notes he made to preserve the location of that cleft in the rocks and he offered them in exchange for his son's life.

"The son was brought to the old man's café by a Colonel Zarb of Egyptian Army Intelligence. Zarb also brought two assistants who were to wait outside the old man's room while the exchange took place. Soiron produced his notes and told his story, and he convinced Zarb that he was speaking the truth. The Egyptian Colonel took the notes, and then calmly announced that it was still not possible to release the son.

"Soiron realised that he had been tricked, and that Zarb had only brought his son along to ensure that the notes were produced. But Zarb had underestimated the old man. Despite the fact that Soiron was in his seventies and handicapped by having only one leg, he was still an ex-sergeant of the Legion, and the Legion had never flinched from hopeless odds. Zarb held a gun, but Soiron died as bravely and in the same tradition as his long dead comrades from blockhouse 38 who had flung themselves in the suicide bayonet charge on the long knives of the Rif. The old legionaire launched himself at the Egyptian Colonel and held him down with two bullets in his chest while his son escaped through the window before Zarb's helpers could break into the room."

There was silence for a long moment, and then Cathy said slowly.

"Who are you? How do you know all this?"

The tall Arab smiled bitterly. "I know because I am the son of that gallant old sergeant of the Legion. I am Kerim Soiron." His mouth hardened and he finished. "And I *want* Colonel Zarb."

16

Pattern of Disaster

Cathy stared at the tall Arab as he finished speaking, and then repeated slowly.

"Kerim. Alan, that's the name Abdullah mentioned at Meknes."

The tall man said quickly, "Who is Abdullah?"

Alan watched him warily as he explained.

"There were two men who cornered us in the old dungeons of Moulay Ismael in Meknes. They wore the hoods of their djellabahs well forward so that it was hard to make out their faces, but they were both tall men, although not quite as tall as you, and they called themselves Mohammed and Abdullah. They said that if we must affix labels then the most common of Arab names would do."

The tall man frowned. "I think they must be Zarb's two assistants. They are both lieutenants in Egyptian Intelligence. Zarb uses them for the less delicate aspects of his work, and they have a preference for using the most ordinary of names."

Cathy said dubiously. "I'm beginning to understand the motives behind all this mystery. But how did my uncle get mixed up in it?"

Kerim shrugged. "I am beginning to think now that your uncle was not mixed up in the matter at all. But his research followed a pattern of disaster that was leading him here to blockhouse 38. I think that if he had not had the misfortune to consult el-Zeba in his search for material then Zarb would have allowed him to live, for it was unlikely that he would have learned anything of importance by a simple visit to the blockhouse itself. It was the coincidence of his visiting el-Zeba and then announcing his intention to visit the blockhouse that caused Zarb to decide that he must be murdered. Zarb had to face the possibility that el-Zeba might have had some idea of the route that caravan intended to take and had passed on some information to Dawson. The Egyptian simply could not afford to have Dawson prying around, however harmless and coincidental his intentions, because there was too strong a risk that he would stumble on to the preparations for removing the spoils from the caravan."

Cathy frowned. "But how would this man Zarb know all about my uncle's intentions?"

Kerim smiled. "Very simply. Zarb rules the main Egyptian Intelligence network throughout the whole of North Africa, his contacts are spread everywhere. Obviously when he came to Morocco to locate and recover the Rif fortune he was able to call upon the complete resources of that network. He made basic enquiries as a matter of routine and discovered that Abd-el-Zeba was the only living survivor of the sheikhs who financed the lost caravan. Naturally he then took the precaution of keeping el-Zeba under observation, most probably by bribing one of the old Sheikh's servants to keep him informed. So when George Dawson appeared and began discussing the Rif wars the information was relayed back to Zarb. Consequently Dawson found it very easy to find a guide who was willing to stay with him for the whole trip, the guide was being paid by Zarb. Dawson informed the guide of his intentions, the guide informed Zarb, and Zarb decided that an accident was very clearly called for. It was arranged with the help of the snake-charmer in the Djemaa el Fina."

Alan was still watching those brilliant black eyes.

"It all sounds plausible," he admitted slowly.

Kerim nodded. "It would all have ended very tidily in the Djemaa el Fina, exactly as Zarb intended, except for the unfortunate fact that you intervened, Mr. Ross. Zarb could not have been sure whether or not Dawson's words were as innocent as you claimed; especially as you began taking what seemed to be an undue interest in the dead man's niece. A man who spends his lifetime in intrigue and searching for hidden answers can sometimes miss the simple fact that became obvious the moment

Miss Dawson believed that you had been hurt; namely that young people of opposite sexes can be attracted solely by love."

Alan felt vaguely embarrassed under the tall man's knowing smile, but he didn't allow the gun in his hand to falter.

He said at last, "So this mysterious Zarb reasoned that Dawson had told me something about the treasure caravan as he died. His two pet killers hinted as much when they cornered us in the dungeons."

"Quite so. I imagine Zarb would have tried to scare you off, just in case you were merely curious and had no idea of what was really at stake."

Alan nodded. "Part of the city wall was pushed down and almost landed on top of us in Marrakech, and then someone threw a knife at us in Casablanca. But I think they had stopped saying boo and were ready to get rough in the dungeons. We were lucky to escape."

"Quite so," Kerim said again. "I think they gave up trying to scare you after you visited el-Zeba. Zarb's two lieutenants must have been close behind you as you left the Sheikh. Your visit convinced them that the old man must have had some information which he had passed on to Dawson and which you wanted to check. So el-Zeba had to be killed. Because you had recognised the guide Achmed he had to be killed also. He was a very minor cog and Zarb had probably employed him to keep an extra watch on el-Zeba when he returned from Marrakech, that was why he was loitering around the Sheikh's home. You young people were very lucky, you were only third and fourth on the murder list and there were only two killers. And you have been lucky since, for it is certain that if those two men, or Zarb, should ever catch up with you then they will kill you out of hand."

Alan found the sweat trickling down his face, and was again aware of the fierce heat of the sun. Cathy was sweating equally freely beside him and the moisture was more pronounced even on Kerim's dark face. The sun was a fiery core in a rippling pool of unbearable heat directly above, but still Alan was unsure of the man in front of him.

He said slowly, "You seem to know an awful lot about Zarb and his intentions. And you seem to have all the answers. If you are running away from the man how can you know so much about him?"

"I am not running from him. I am trying to find him. I told you that I was sentenced to death by the Cairo Government for spying on behalf of the Americans. That was true. I am also in the espionage business, and I also have my contacts throughout North Africa. Like Zarb I have no scruples about using those contacts for my own ends. Zarb killed my father and I intend to find him. I knew that the lure of the Rif fortune would bring him to Morocco, and so I was able to get here ahead of him. I have been able to keep track of his two lieutenants, but so far Zarb himself has been fortunate enough to avoid me. However, the reports of my contacts and my own knowledge of Zarb's methods and the precautions he would take have enabled me to maintain what I am sure is a reasonably accurate picture of his progress."

Alan was conscious of that pitiless sun again, and knew that he should have the sense to continue the conversation in the shade.

Instead he said, "Why are you here now?"

The tall man's mouth shaped the position of a smile, but this time that was all.

"I am here because at any moment I am expecting Zarb and his two lieutenants to arrive. I know that all three spent last night in Zagora, and that eventually they must come here."

Cathy stared. "But we were in Zagora last night."

"I know that too, but fortunately you both went straight to an hotel and stayed there. The Egyptians missed you. Possibly they are still there waiting for you, and probably for me, to arrive. They want all the awkward ends tied up before they can actually try to locate the fortune. But eventually they must come here — and I will be waiting for them."

Alan stared into the man's face, his mind searching the whole story for the signs of a flaw. There were none. He recalled the man Cathy had seen in Ouarzazate, the knifethrower from Casablanca. That unknown man must have been Zarb, and as he had been in Ouarzazate during the afternoon it was quite likely that he had reached Zagora by night. Despite himself Alan was beginning to believe the tall man's story.

Kerim said at last. "I think you now know everything, Mr. Ross. And as our enemies are liable to appear at any moment I think perhaps we had best sign a truce." He lowered his hands confidently and added, "I am more accustomed to fire-arms — can you trust me enough to return my gun?"

Alan lowered the automatic but did not return it.

"There's no rush."

"But perhaps there is, Mr. Ross. This is not your job, and it is most definitely no place for Miss Dawson. I would suggest that you relinquished the gun and then instruct your driver to get you both as far away from these ruins as possible. But do not return to Zagora. Go instead to Mhamid and wait there."

"It's not as simple as that. The police are still hunting for us in the belief that I killed Achmed and el-Zeba."

Kerim shrugged. "That is now the least of your worries. The police can hardly continue believing that now that you can give them the full story. All I ask is that you wait forty-eight hours in Mhamid to give me a chance to settle with Zarb before you contact the police. You must understand that my father gave his life for me — I must avenge him personally."

Alan said dubiously, "You're one man against three. I don't like the idea of running out on you."

"I am quite capable." The statement was not a boast but a simple fact. "Your. loyalty lies with Miss Dawson. You must get her to safety. Were you alone I would accept your help, but when Zarb comes I will kill him, and death is not a pretty thing for a young lady to see."

Alan wavered, and then Kerim glanced

up and acknowledged the blazing fire of the sun for the first time.

"If we must still talk," he said, "then let us get inside the blockhouse walls and attempt to find some shade. This heat is killing me."

Alan stiffened as the tall Arab turned towards the narrow gateway through the nine foot wall, then he relaxed and let the gun in his hand fall back to his side. He looked down at Cathy and she nodded briefly. Together they moved to follow Kerim and Alan felt suddenly faint from the effects of standing bare-headed in the sun. Cathy swayed against him. Then there was an abrupt shout from the half forgotten Arshid.

Kerim twisted in the gateway and came back fast, both hands moving up to form a bridge over his eyes. Arshid's exclamation had been in French but the gesture of the outflung arm was self-explanatory and Alan swiftly copied Kerim's example.

Blockhouse 38 was built on high ground to command a wide view. Six hundred yards away, below and to their left, lay the lush green oval of the oasis. To the left of the oasis ran the faintly discernible line of the camel track they had followed in the Land Rover, running past and then looping round to the main gateway to the fort. Left of the track where Arshid's finger was pointing there was nothing but rippling wastes of sand stretching far to the heat-warped shimmer of the horizon.

Alan squeezed his eyes shut, rubbed the sweat away, and then looked again.

Kerim said slowly. "I think — yes — it's a camel rider."

Alan squeezed his eyes up a second time, and with the third attempt he too saw the distant black speak far out in the desert. It was far to the left so that he had to stare almost along the line of the wall and crumbling corner tower of the blockhouse before he could find it. He watched it for a moment, accepting Kerim's identification without being able to distinguish any features for himself. Then he had to close his aching eyes again.

Kerim snapped sharply. "Not one

rider — three. There are two more specks on the horizon behind him." He spun round to face them and finished more calmly. "It can only be Zarb and his two companions. They are coming from the right direction."

Alan looked down at the comforting shape of the gun in his hand. Then said grimly, "What do we do now."

"First get back in the blockhouse out of sight. It is too late now for you and Miss Dawson to make your escape — but we have several minutes to prepare. They are still a long way off."

"Then you'd better have this."

The time for hesitation was over and Alan flipped the automatic towards Kerim, the tall Arab caught it neatly, thrust it into the waistband of his breeches and then turned into the fort. Alan and Cathy followed while the bewildered Arshid chose that moment to ask the rush of questions that must have been storing up in his nervous brain for the last hour. Cathy started to say something in French and then Kerim rapped a curt command in Arabic that silenced Arshid completely.

Kerim glanced swiftly around the inside of the fort and his gaze stopped on the parked Land Rover.

"We must get that vehicle out of sight, or at least pushed against the wall where it will not be seen until they actually ride in through the gateway. Quickly now." He barked another order in Arabic for Arshid's benefit and then ran with long, thrusting strides towards the Land Rover.

Alan and Cathy ran after him, and the reluctant Arshid followed at slower speed. The Arab's black-button eyes glared at Kerim's back and with the pouting effect of his bushy moustache made him look more petulant than ever.

They reached the Land Rover and all four bent their backs to the task of pushing it over to the wall. The sweating task took them several minutes and before it was over Kerim sent Cathy to the gateway to keep watch. The three men finished the job in a final surge of effort that forced the stubborn wheels through the soft sand.

Cathy stood in the shadow of the

gateway with her shoulders flat against the wall. She said clearly,

"They are about half-way here now. One of them is well in lead of the other two and they are coming very fast."

Kerim ran to join her and Alan was less than a pace behind. The distant, shimmering outlines of the three camel riders were almost half life-size now, and looking larger. The leader had a good start and the other two were close together. Kerim uttered a burst of Arabic which by its violence could only have been an oath, and then he pulled Cathy back inside the fort. Alan ducked back out of sight with them.

The tall Arab pulled the heavy black automatic from his waistband and said grimly.

"This is going to be awkward. I had hoped that they would all be together, but if Zarb rides in only half a minute ahead then any noise in securing him will warn the other two. Your driver seems to be absolutely useless, Mr. Ross, so it looks as though I must accept your offer

298

of help. That is if it is still open."

Alan glanced across at Arshid who had remained nervously by his battered Land Rover, his arms stiffly by his sides and a nervous expression on his face, and saw that Kerim was right.

He said quickly, "The offer is still open. What can I do."

"Distract Zarb's attention for me. Get behind the sand humps that mark the remains of the barracks and just stand up in full view as Zarb rides in. I will be on the firing platform on the wall and as he faces you he will have his back to me. As the Americans would say, I will have the drop on him. Abdullah and Mohammed will ride in behind him and at first sight it will appear that he is merely confronting you, it will enable me to cover them also."

Alan nodded and turned to Cathy.

"Get in the car with Arshid," he ordered. "And keep your head down."

"No. I'll keep with you. They'll expect us to be together." She saw the signs of argument flash into his face and killed them defiantly. "There isn't time

299

to squabble, damn you. They're almost here."

Alan began angrily. "No, Cathy. I won't — "

"Do as she says, Mr. Ross. There's no time."

Kerim gave them both a push and then turned and ran to the wall. He clamped the heavy automatic in his teeth for an instant as he pulled himself up on to the firing platform that ran along the parapet. He crouched there on his knees, ten yards to the right of the gateway, transferring the gun smoothly back into his right hand as he squinted out across the sweeping sands. He turned and urgently waved them down.

There was no time left. Arshid had already scrambled into the dubious safety of his Land Rover and was cowering low. Alan turned and ran out into the centre of the enclosure with Cathy at his heels, and dragged her down into a concealing hollow behind the humped foundations of what had once been part of the barracks. They were slightly to the left of the gateway but could see straight through it.

There was sudden, deathly silence inside the ruined walls of the desert outpost. Arshid was hidden from view, and Kerim was motionless as he knelt on the firing platform. There was not even a breath of wind to disturb the white burnous that was fastened around his forehead and spread loosely across his shoulders like a cloak. The one standing corner tower stood like a lonely sentry against the savage blue of the sky, and the now westering sun threw saw-toothed shadows from the fortress walls.

Alan lay on his stomach with Cathy face down beside him, his arm stretched across her shoulders to pin her down. The sand was burning hot where it touched their bare flesh and the sun flayed at their backs. He could feel the sweat soaking out of him, and as he glanced at Cathy he could see the glistening trails of moisture moving inside her blouse in the deep cleft of her breasts. It was the first time he had ever consciously looked in that direction and he suddenly realised that this was a most bizarre moment to start.

He looked back at the still empty

gateway, his muscles tense in the hushed silence. Overhead the sky was also empty, but he would not have been surprised to see vultures hovering. It suddenly occurred to him to wonder whether Kerim really did mean to hold his enemy at gun-point, or whether he would cold-bloodedly shoot him in the back. But it was too late to voice any doubts.

The silence blossomed into action with an unexpected speed that sent limp fear quivering like a delicious pain throughout the whole of Alan's body. Cathy went rigid beside him as the first of the approaching camel riders swept completely without warning through the gateway. The soft sand had muffled the camel's footsteps and even as it came rushing into the fortress the flying hooves kicked up the yellow clouds with a minimum of noise. The rider was crouched well forward on the single high hump, the reins in one hand and the other gripping a gleaming rifle. The brute tore straight towards them and the sight galvanised Alan into frantic life, rolling

Cathy desperately out of its way. The rider was already throwing his weight backwards to drag his runaway mount to a roaring stop.

The camel reared, its huge mouth wide and snarling through vicious teeth and flabby lips. The rider fought desperately to control it as Alan and Cathy sprang to their feet, and both of them recognised him in the same instant.

It was the man who had thrown the knife in Casablanca.

That was when Kerim stood fully upright on the firing platform and roared a command.

The camel rider twisted in his saddle to face the threat at his back, desperately trying to bring his rifle to bear. He yelled one frantic unbelieving word.

"Zarb!"

And then the tall Arab on the parapet fired the heavy black automatic and the camel rider was knocked clean off the animal's back.

Alan stared at the black automatic and realised the full enormity of his mammoth mistake.

17

The Twists of Fate

The plunging camel twisted away from its fallen rider, its long bony legs flashing like pistons into the sand and its eyes crazed with fear. It bolted and narrowly missed trampling both Alan and Cathy underfoot. It wheeled in a frantic sand-spraying circle inside the blockhouse, searching blindly for an exit through the decaying walls. It failed to find the gateway through which it had entered and slowly cantered to a halt.

Alan steadied Cathy as the camel ran itself to a stop, and then he stared again at the tall Arab on the parapet. The camel's rider sprawled in a painfully twisting heap only six yards away, and four yards away lay the gleaming rifle that had been loosened from his hand. The rifle was half buried in the sand that had been churned up as the camel ran wild, and Alan made a desperate attempt to reach it, thrusting Cathy aside and down on to the sand as he did so.

The tall Arab on the parapet roared a warning and lifted the automatic. Alan froze on one knee with his outstretched fingers almost touching the rifle, and then in that moment Abdullah and Mohammed swept through the gateway, hauling up their camels amid curtains of sand and levelling their rifles.

Alan licked his lips and tasted the sweat that was running down from his forehead to drench his face. Slowly, like a man cornered in a cage full of wild beasts, he backed away.

Cathy struggled to her feet and pressed close beside him, staring up at the two camel riders who were now relaxed and grinning. Then she looked at the tall Arab who still threatened them with the automatic from the wall. Helplessly her eyes moved to Alan's face.

"Alan — Alan, I don't understand."

Alan said bitterly, "But I do. The man we just helped to trap addressed our tall friend as Zarb. We were told a

305

very plausible story, and I don't doubt that it was all perfectly true — except for a slight exchange of identities. The man who told it and introduced himself as Kerim is really Zarb."

His explanation also helped to enlighten the two men still seated on their camels, for despite their grins and the fact that they had everything under control there was a hint of puzzlement in their expressions that showed that they were not quite clear now how it had all come about. Mohammed shifted in his saddle to look at the tall man with the automatic and said,

"So we catch them all together, hey, Colonel? This is really fortunate."

The man they had called Kerim, now definitely identified as the Egyptian Colonel Zarb, said calmly,

"Quite so, Lieutenant. As Mr. Ross has said, it was simply a matter of exchanging identities."

The fallen rider of the first camel was now struggling to his knees in the sand, his right hand clutching at his left shoulder where red stains were already marring the whiteness of his shirt and the cloak-like burnous. Alan was relieved to see that the man was alive and moved to help him.

The injured man looked up, pain and bitterness reflected in his ageless face. The steel sharp eyes were blurred but his mind still functioned. He said quickly, "Don't get too close to the rifle."

Alan looked up and saw what the man on the sand had sensed. Abdullah's rifle was raised and within a hair's breadth of sending a bullet crashing into his chest. Slowly Alan looked down at the rifle near his feet, and very carefully he hooked one foot under it and kicked it clear. Abdullah smiled broadly and relaxed again. Zarb nodded to Mohammed who swung down from his camel's back and came forward to collect the fallen rifle from the sand.

Alan helped the man with the wounded shoulder to his feet. The man's dark face was as much European as Arab, and he could see the signs of French blood. He should have realised that a man as dark as the watching killer on the wall behind them could only be a full-blooded Arab.

He should have realised too that the three camel riders had been pursuers and pursued, and not separated companions. It was clear now why Zarb had bundled himself and Cathy away from the gateway before they realised too much. He knew how inadequate his words were going to sound and said weakly,

"It's pretty obvious now that you must be the real Kerim Soiron. I'm damned sorry that we let you in for this."

Cathy was still uncertain. She said hesitantly,

"But Alan, he is the one who tried to kill us in Casablanca. I remember him clearly. And he was in Ouarzazate."

The wounded man smiled faintly. "I didn't try to kill you, Miss Dawson, but merely to frighten you. I am an excellent shot with a knife and the one that stuck exactly between your two heads was meant to stick there and nowhere else. I hoped to scare you away, partly because I did not want your interference hampering my own efforts, and partly because I did not want to see you both permanently removed by Zarb's more drastic methods.

As you have seen, the Egyptian Colonel has no finesse."

Mohammed had now picked up the fallen rifle and was levelling it at them only a few yards away, his own weapon he had left on his camel. Zarb dropped down from the firing platform on the wall and came towards them. Abdullah dismounted.

Zarb said briskly, "There is an Arab driver hiding in the Land Rover. You had best fetch him out where we can see him."

Abdullah nodded and went over to the Land Rover. He poked the barrel of his rifle inside and prodded without any gentleness. There was a chorus of yelps and whimpers and finally the reluctant Arshid was flushed out and herded over to join the rest of the prisoners.

Kerim Soiron was now standing upright, and apart from clasping his wounded arm his stance and face showed nothing of his feelings as the tall Zarb stopped in front of him. The Egyptian smiled and then looked at Alan.

"Do not feel so badly, Mr. Ross. If

309

you and Miss Dawson had not been here the unfortunate Kerim would still have rode straight into my hands. Far from helping me your presence provided a problem, the problem of keeping you quiet while he blundered into the trap I had to improvise so hastily."

Alan said harshly, "So, what happens now?"

"Nothing that would not have happened before. You have already guessed that apart from exchanging identities I told you the truth about this blockhouse and the Rif fortune. I had to tell the truth because it would have been impossible to make up a convincing enough story that would include all the answers you needed to leave you satisfied. Of course once I had convinced you and you had returned my automatic I intended to kill you both, and your snivelling driver, because obviously I could not allow that story to go any further. Kerim's arrival was completely unexpected, but although it induced you to return my gun more swiftly it also meant that I had to postpone shooting you or he would have heard the shots and sheered off." A thought occurred to the tall Arab and he turned sharply upon his two lieutenants. "Why was Kerim allowed to get this far, you were ordered to stop him in Zagora?"

Mohammed stiffened, his shoulders bracing to attention.

"It was because the traitor did not come through Zagora, Colonel. We waited as you ordered after the report that he was in Ouarzazate, but then began to suspect that he may have hired a camel at one of the Kasbahs along the road. It was quite possible that he would expect a trap in Zagora and try to avoid the town."

Mohammed paused for breath and Abdullah continued.

"We drove back towards Ouarzazate, Colonel. Mohammed stayed with the car to watch the road while I enquired in each village. We eventually found that the traitor had hired a camel in one of them and was only an hour ahead of us. So we hired fresh camels and followed. We rode fast but could not catch him until we were almost upon the blockhouse."

Zarb smiled. "Then you did well."

Cathy was watching the blood that trickled over Kerim's fingers where he clutched his arm. Her face was pale but she said bravely,

"Can't we do something for that arm?"

Zarb stared at her and laughed, his teeth flashing whitely in his amused mouth. Abdullah and Mohammed allowed themselves slow grins.

Cathy flinched at their reactions and pressed closer to Alan.

Then Kerim looked at her and said quietly, "It is a kind thought, Miss Dawson, but a pointless one. I am afraid that Zarb will not allow any of us to live. I am very sorry."

Alan looked at Kerim's face, there was neither hope nor defeat there, but simply a plain acceptance of the facts. The Egyptian was in complete control and he obviously could not afford to let any of them live.

Alan could feel a quivering sensation creeping into his bunched muscles, it was not fear, but more a blind mounting anger. The thought of Cathy reeling under the impact of a bullet from one of the two rifles that faced them was a pain that washed out all thought of the agony of his own death, a pain that goaded a deep and burning hatred for the three Egyptians. But Zarb watched him with unblinking eyes, knowing that in desperation the young Englishman was far more dangerous than any trained man, giving him no chance at all.

Under the brilliant black gaze of Zarb's watching eyes Alan slowly controlled the fit of approaching madness. Instead he searched desperately for some measure of help. There was none. Mohammed kept his rifle safely trained on Kerim's stomach from a gap of seven feet, while Abdullah watched warily over the trembling Arshid. Alan began to believe that Arshid would be as likely to die of fear as to fight anyway.

There was nothing more to be said except the last order, but still the moment was drawn out beneath the blistering sun. Alan felt as though every single inch of his skin was pouring out sweat, and the back of Cathy's blouse beneath his encircling

313

arm was sodden. The only sound was her breathing, and the only movement the uneven motion of her breasts.

Then slowly Zarb smiled, and carefully backed away. He confidently pushed the automatic into his waist band and then nodded to his two lieutenants.

"Finish it quickly."

Mohammed lifted his rifle, its aim settling on Kerim's heart. And then Abdullah said hesitantly,

"Wait!"

Zarb stiffened in surprise, opened his mouth to say something, and then stopped, listening. There was another eternity of silence and then Alan heard it too; the faint sound of a car engine out in the desert.

Zarb swore and ran towards the blockhouse wall. He scrambled up quickly on to the firing platform behind the parapet and stared through the embrasure. He swore again with rising fury.

"It's a jeep," he called back to his two men. "And it looks like a damned police jeep, coming up the camel track past the oasis."

"It is a police jeep." The completely new voice spoke with savage authority. "And this is a police revolver. And I will ask you exactly once to throw those weapons on to the sand."

18

The Oasis of Revenge

Both Mohammed and Abdullah had backed away to a safe distance at the first sign of the interruption to await fresh orders from their Colonel. Their interest was fixed on Zarb as he knelt on the wall and on the sound of the approaching engine, Alan and Cathy were similarly distracted. The heads of all four were jerked round as though flicked by an invisible whip. Zarb, too, pivoted desperately on the firing platform.

The identity of that mystery voice was as startling and unexpected as the sound of its first biting command. Arshid was no longer snivelling, no longer dejected, his shoulders no longer hunched. Instead he stood perfectly upright, his feet braced and his shoulders steady. The black button eyes were no longer bewildered and the bushy moustache had lost its pouting effect on a mouth that had gone straight and hard. The heavy police revolver in his hand was directed at a stomach-level spot exactly between Zarb's two lieutenants.

There was an infinitesimal instant of frozen time and then Abdullah twisted his rifle back to bear and fired. Arshid saw the first vicious contraction of the facial muscles and flicked the big revolver sideways to blast off one shot before the Egyptian's finger could fully complete the trigger pressure. Abdullah screamed over the combined reports, his mouth bursting open and his doubled body crashing backwards as the bullet kicked deep into his stomach. Arshid spun round in the same instant as the rifle bullet slammed into his thigh.

Both men hit the sand, but where Abdullah lay still and contorted in death Arshid was still very much alive, the big revolver already covering Mohammed.

Kerim, the only one to have remained fully alert, was already in action. Ignoring his wounded shoulder his left hand was grabbing for Mohammed's rifle. He

317

snatched it away as his right fist smashed in a murderous blow to the man's jaw that knocked him sprawling beside his dead companion.

Arshid switched his attention immediately to the last threat. On the parapet Zarb had already snatched the automatic from his waistband and his arm was fully extended for maximum accuracy. The shot tore up a flurry of sand beside Arshid's head and then the big police revolver blasted for the second time. Plaster cascaded away from the splintering wall beside Zarb's hip.

For a second the tall Egyptian Colonel stood there, and the sound of the jeep racing up the camel track came clearly above the echoes of the shots that rang through the block-house walls. Zarb fired a final shot and then vaulted clean over the wall out of sight.

Alan struggled desperately to his feet. At the sound of the first shot he had acted on blind instinct, throwing Cathy down on the sand and sprawling protectively on top of her. Now he felt slightly ashamed that it had been left to the wounded Kerin to back the fallen Arshid.

Arshid was now keeping the big revolver carefully trained on Mohammed, his hand still steady despite the pain that contorted his face.

"Let the Colonel run," he said grimly. "He will not get far."

Kerim had transferred the rifle to his right hand.

"I'll get him," he said harshly. *"Zarb is mine!"*

He turned and ran swiftly through the gateway.

Alan hesitated, and then he lunged forward and picked up the fallen rifle that had belonged to the dead Abdullah.

"Stay here," he told Cathy. "Look after Arshid. I'm going after Kerim."

He twisted away from her faltering gaze and ran swiftly towards the gateway. He heard her shout and ignored it, ignoring, too, an angry order from Arshid. He only knew that Kerim was wounded and attempting to hunt down a killer. There was no time to wait until the rest of the police arrived. For he was realising now that Arshid could only be a policeman. He was remembering too how Zarb had callously prepared to watch Cathy shot down by his two thugs, and that made it personal for him too.

The sound of a rifle shot made him flinch as he reached the gateway, but there was no sign of either Zarb or Kerim. He hesitated and then realised that there was only one place that Zarb would make for. He turned and ran swiftly along the wall towards the high corner tower, noticing the deep disturbance in the sand where the Egyptian had jumped down from the nine foot wall and following the footprints that marked his path. He heard Cathy shout again behind him and knew without looking round that she had followed him out of the fort.

He reached the projecting corner tower and ran round it blindly, halting and tightening his grip upon his rifle as his view was widened. Below was the oasis, and heading for it at a fast zig-zagging run was the tall figure of Zarb. A hundred yards behind him was Kerim, then in the act of dropping on to one knee in the sand and bringing his rifle up to his sound right shoulder. The French-Egyptian fired, but Zarb made a fast dodging target and the wounded left shoulder was obviously affecting Kerim's aim. The shot went wide.

The police jeep was still a distant snarling toy on the camel track beyond the oasis, the sound of it carrying sharp and clear through the hot desert air. Zarb was three-quarters of the way to the oasis and increasing his lead. Alan heard Cathy flounder round the side of the blockhouse beside him and yelled at her to go back. Her wide honey-brown eyes looked uncertain and hurt as she stopped dead and stared at him, afraid of the grim rage that had transformed him completely. And then he left her standing and ploughed down the sandy slope to join Kerim.

"He's got a camel in the oasis," he shouted warningly. "Don't let him reach it."

Kerim must have heard but he spared no time for answering, simply increasing his speed as he raced after Zarb. He made no more efforts to bring down the running man, knowing that he was too handicapped to score a hit and concentrating on an attempt to close the gap. Zarb, armed with only the automatic dared not stop to provide a target, and trusted to his long legs to take him to safety.

Alan slowly gained on Kerim, throwing every energy into the chase. The sun was still scorching down from the western sky and the more distant figure of Zarb was becoming indistinct in the haze of heat. Sweat was streaming down Alan's face and blurring his sight even more. He caught up with the floundering Kerim as Zarb vanished into the green fringe of the oasis a hundred and fifty yards ahead.

Behind them Cathy was making a stumbling effort to catch up, the fear for Alan and the blanketing heat smothering all other thoughts from her mind.

Kerim swerved off his direct course but continued his breakneck speed. He was too well trained to make the suicide move of following Zarb through the same gap in the palms, but knew he had to make cover swiftly before the Egyptian could realise that he had changed course and cut through the greenery to lay an ambush. Alan stayed blindly by Kerim's side and together they raced beneath the palms and jerked to a halt.

There was no sign of Zarb. They were surrounded by a miniature jungle of palms, cacti, tangled bushes and brilliant red and white blossoms. It could have been paradise in the desert but for the circumstances of their being here.

Kerim stood listening, the rifle levelled in his hands and the large red stain showing predominantly on his left shoulder. Alan stood breathlessly beside him, equally alert.

"Where is the camel?" Kerim asked softly.

"I don't know. I just know that there is one."

They heard the sound of the jeep tearing past the oasis and heading for the fort. Kerim ignored it, his eyes fixed on Alan's.

"You should go back, Mr. Ross. This is my job. Colonel Zarb very cold-bloodedly tricked and murdered my father, an old one-legged man who had no chance against him."

"I know." Alan's voice became harsh. "But ten minutes ago he was prepared to equally cold-bloodedly murder us all."

Quite unexpectedly Kerim smiled. "By all you undoubtedly mean Miss Dawson. It is plain that to you she means all." He glanced at the red stain on his own shoulder admitting for the first time that it was there. Then he finished. "Glad to have you along, Mr. Ross. Isn't that what you English say?"

He didn't wait for an answer but began to move forward slowly, his gaze searching through the foliage beneath the shading fronds of the palms.

He murmured very softly, "No more talking, Mr. Ross. Keep absolute silence."

Alan obeyed. His mouth was tight and he could count every violently erratic beat of his thudding heart as he kept pace with the grim French-Egyptian, but there was still a cold determination and his own anger to keep him going. He was afraid, but the memory of Zarb's smile when he had ordered his lieutenants to kill them all conquered his fear. The agony of mind when he had expected to watch Cathy die still prevailed, and only the Egyptian Colonel's death would ease it.

Kerim was an avenging shadow beside him, equally dedicated that Zarb should die. They were penetrating soundlessly towards the centre of the oasis, and Alan guessed that Kerim was making for the deep well of clear water that gave life to the lush setting around them. The well was the most likely place for the camel to stay content.

He wondered whether Zarb was concentrating on the camel and escape, or whether the tall Arab harboured his own thoughts of vengeance at the loss of his two lieutenants and the ruination of his plans. It was a stomach-gnawing thought. Were they still the hunters, or were they now the hunted in this pocket jungle of green and shadows? Was Zarb still running, or was he lying in wait now that the close confines of their surroundings would allow them to walk unwittingly into close range where the automatic would be as effective as the two rifles? In fact the automatic would be more effective, for Zarb was the expert whereas Kerim was slowed by his wound and Alan was a complete stranger to firearms.

The rifle in Alan's hands was wet and slippery, as though filmed with fine oil, then he realised that it was not oil but sweat from his palms. It was cooler here beneath the trees, shielded from the hot stab of the sun, but the sweat was still running off him like grease from melting butter.

There was a splinter of pale blue through the barrier of green. Kerim became motionless, half kneeling on the sand. Alan froze behind him, every muscle tensed to screaming pitch. There was no sound, not even a bird in the fronds and branches above. A spiky cactus with disc-like growths on its stumpy arms threw a shadow like the warped figure of a man that brought fear jumping into Alan's throat. The fear was controlled only to rush back again as a nervous snorting sound came from ahead.

Kerim was moving again, inching his way forward without disturbing a single branch, his sandles brushing gently and silently across the sand. Alan moved with him. He passed close to the cactus and a needle-sharp spike scratched across his face. The spike traced a thin red line but he did not even notice. Ahead the splinter of blue was becoming wider, taking the shape of a pool. The nervous, hissing snort came again and a heavy body shifted and rustled the branches near the water's edge.

Alan saw the camel's head, the neck craned high as the brute searched suspiciously. The very silence had alarmed it, or perhaps it had caught their scent on the slight breeze. They moved closer and saw the shape of the hump through the bushes and the high, ornamented leather saddle. The camel's reins were looped around a palm trunk on the edge of a wide sandy clearing that had the clear blue well in its centre.

Kerim sank down to his knees, his dark face blank and grim.

Alan knelt beside him and they

exchanged glances that showed that both were fully aware of the position. Zarb had made no attempt to simply jump on his camel and flee, the tall Arab intended to kill them first. The rifle in Alan's unskilled hands was no longer reassuring, and neither was the red stain on Kerim's shoulder that was slowly, but very surely spreading down his arm. Kerim's face showed no sign of pain, but Alan knew that it was there, kept only by the strongest effort below the surface.

Kerim's lips framed two words, "We wait."

Alan knew that he was right. The sound of the jeep's engine had stopped in the direction of the blockhouse, and it was certain that Arshid would send his colleagues hurrying to the oasis to support them. Time was on their side and Zarb's only hope was his camel and flight across the desert. If Zarb was hunting them then he would have to make the first moves and fast. The odds were delicately balanced but still slightly in their favour.

They had forgotten completely about Cathy, for neither of them had looked behind as they had plunged into the oasis. She was still only half-way across the open stretch of desert from the fort as they vanished and she blundered after them blindly in an effort to catch up with Alan.

She stumbled into the fringe of palms and there she stopped, gasping for breath. She stood uncertainly against one of the slim bare trunks, staring around her and wondering which way they had gone. She had entered the oasis at a different point and there were no footprints in the sand to guide her. There was no sound and the bright green maze of palms and other vegetation became abruptly menacing.

For the first time she began to think and realised the foolishness of her action, but now it was too late. She was afraid to go back into the wide open desert where there was no place to hide. Instead she moved hesitantly deeper into the oasis. She heard the police jeep go screeching past along the camel track, but dared not make any sound.

Zarb, who had halted immediately on reaching the palms, had watched all three of his enemies sprint the last hundred yards. If he had not seen Cathy behind them he would have dashed through the fringe of concealing greenery to intercept the two men, but the girl showed every sign of continuing her blind progress and he knew that he could afford to wait. There was no need to risk the threat of the two rifles, even though he doubted that either of his pursuers could fire straight.

He allowed Cathy to move deeper into the oasis and then caught her easily, stepping up behind her and hooking one powerful arm around her throat.

Alan heard Cathy's piercing scream and sprang frantically to his feet, swinging back to face the way they had come. Then Kerim's left hand clamped on his shoulder. Alan twisted and then stopped as he saw the increasing rush of red pumping down Kerim's arm.

"Easy, Mr. Ross. For God's sake."

Kerim released his grip and his face was now white.

Then Zarb's voice rang sharp and loud through the palms.

"Soiron! Mr. Ross I have the girl. At the moment the nose of my automatic is pressing hard into her left ear. Even if you shoot me down from hiding my reflexes will blast her brains out through the opposite side of her head. I am sure you will not want that."

Alan's agony of mind kept him rooted to the spot. It was Kerim who answered.

"We hear you, Zarb. What do you want?"

"Simply to escape. I don't doubt that you are waiting for me by my camel. I shall approach the animal with Miss Dawson. Remember that if I die — she dies."

Kerim hesitated. When he shouted back his voice was tinged with bitterness.

"You win, Zarb. Your life isn't worth the girl's. But there'll be another day. Neither of us will attempt to shoot."

There was a pause, and the sound of distant branches being pushed aside as Zarb approached. The need for silence was absent now and the rustlings grew louder until Zarb appeared through the close-packed palms. The heavy black automatic in his hand looked as large and lethal as a twelve-bore as it pressed against Cathy's ear. Her face was white and she walked awkwardly with Zarb's left arm clamping her shoulders to his chest.

"Back up, Soiron. And you, Mr. Ross." The Egyptian's tone invited no argument. "Get over by the pool where I can see both of you clearly."

Kerim's hand closed over Alan's arm despite the wrench of pain the movement caused in his shoulder.

"Do as he says, Mr. Ross. He isn't playing."

Alan had eyes only for Cathy's face. He moved like an automaton as Kerim led him slowly backwards to the edge of the large pool of clear blue water that bubbled up from the desert well.

Zarb was smiling, and there was a minimum of sweat on his dark features.

"The rifles," he snapped. "Throw them into the pool — as far away from you as you can."

For the first time Kerim hesitated, and then he half turned and hurled his rifle into the clear waters. It hit with a splash that created dazzling silver patterns in the sunlight, and then slowly it sank to the bottom. Alan wavered only from a reluctance to make any move at all, and then he followed suit. The second rifle sank beside the first.

Zarb relaxed. "Excellent, perhaps I shall not have to kill Miss Dawson after all."

He moved past them slowly, the automatic still boring hard against Cathy's ear. He didn't come too close and took no chances, backing carefully towards his camel. The animal watched him as warily as the two men with their backs to the pool as he approached. Zarb reached the palm tree beside his mount and stopped.

He said calmly, "Don't attempt to move, Miss Dawson. Don't even faint."

His left arm released her slowly and she swallowed hard. For a moment it seemed that she would fall without his help and then she stood steady. Zarb smiled and used his left hand to untie the reins of the camel.

There was nothing that either Kerim or Alan could do but watch. The tall Egyptian turned the camel round so that he could remain facing them as he mounted, the automatic in his hand remaining always levelled at Cathy's head. There was a short cane hanging by a loop from the high saddle and Zarb took it down with his left hand. He uttered a sharp command and rapped the camel smartly across the base of the neck at the same time. The brute shifted away. A trace of sweat appeared on Zarb's face and he struck again, repeating the command. Slowly the camel folded up at the knees, its back remaining arched in the air while the ugly head sank down towards the sand. Zarb smiled as pleasantly as a tiger shark.

Another sharp whack with the cane, this time across the rump, and the camel was kneeling as low as it could get. Zarb replaced the cane on the saddle and gripped Cathy's shoulder, the black snout of the gun thrusting against her ear again. She flinched but had no choice except to go with him as he backed up until he was touching the camel's hump.

"I'm sorry, Miss Dawson, but you'll have to ride with me for a short while. The police will be here at any moment and they have three camels in the blockhouse with which to make pursuit. I might need a hostage." He saw Alan start blindly forward and rapped curtly. "Back, Mr. Ross! I don't need you."

Alan stopped in his tracks, staring with wretched anguish at Cathy's face. If he could have died to help her then he knew that he would have done so, but he also knew that his dying would not help.

Zarb began the awkward task of mounting the kneeling camel, awkward because he would not risk using either hand. It took him several slow moments to get astride the saddle and then he ordered Cathy to mount in front of him. When she was seated he reached forward with one long leg and kicked his heel against the side of the animal's neck as he shouted the command to rise. The camel's hump swayed as it lurched upwards but the automatic was ever steady against Cathy's ear as Zarb held her in front of him. Cathy's hands appeared to be clasped to her middle as though the fear in her stomach was causing her physical pain.

The camel was upright and Zarb's tigerish smile appeared again.

"This is where I leave you, my friends. But first I have a small parting gift for each of you."

The Egyptian's arm straightened like an accusing finger, the black automatic aiming straight for Kerim. Alan realised that another second and the man beside him would die, and then it would be his own turn. And then Cathy's hand moved in a lightning swift throwing gesture towards the camel's nose. A scrap of white unfurled directly below the brute's huge, flaring nostrils and a faint cloud floated upwards.

The camel almost blew its own head off with one almighty sneeze, its body bucking violently with the unexpected explosion. Both Zarb and Cathy were spilled from its rearing back to go crashing on to the sand.

Cathy rolled clear and Alan dived towards Zarb like a man possessed. But the distance was too great and Zarb too fast. The Egyptian Colonel was on his knees and still hanging on to his gun, his hand bringing it up and already tightening for the shot that would blast the Englishman aside.

And then Kerim screamed.

"Zarb!"

The Egyptian swung to face the new threat, and even Alan turned at the triumph and fury in that screaming voice. Kerim's face was a savage mask as his hand reappeared from a diving movement inside his robes. His arm flashed forward and the fingers splayed in the same smooth movement that Alan had seen before in the medina at Casablanca, except that this time the knife was not meant to miss. It flashed past Alan's face in a blur of silver and buried deep and true in the centre of Zarb's chest. The Egyptian swayed on his knees, loosed one dying bullet harmlessly into the sand, and then slowly fell.

19

Walk into the Sunset

The roaring camel had already bolted through the palms, flinging its ugly head from side to side as though in utmost agony and still blowing through its nostrils in tortured sneezes. Alan stared down at the crumpled figure of Zarb, and behind him Kerim finally gave way to his pain and sank down on to his knees, his head bowed as he clutched at his red-stained arm below the shoulder wound. Alan felt as though events had overtaken him and left him standing now that Zarb was dead, and then his thoughts rushed back to Cathy and he hurried to her side.

He knelt beside her as she attempted to push herself up from the sand and pulled her violently into his arms, as though even now there might be still some threat to part them. She clung to him with desperate urgency, as though she too could not quite believe that they were together and alive. Her body trembled uncontrollably and she half sobbed as she fought for breath with her face against his chest. He kissed her hair and caressed her until eventually they heard the sound of men shouting and crashing towards them through the palms.

He helped her stand and said at last, "What on earth did you do to that camel?"

"Pepper," she laughed almost hysterically. "Just pepper." She sobered slightly in his fast embrace and blinked away the traces of tears that had appeared with the gold flecks in her honey-brown eyes. "Do you remember the dungeons in Meknes? The pepper worked so well there that I bought some more at the next opportunity, which was while I was waiting for you to turn up in Marrakech. Only this time I kept it in the little waist pocket in my jeans. Zarb didn't give me any chance to use it because he kept behind me. So I threw it under the camel's nose."

"Poor bloody camel," said Alan, and

he kissed her again.

A moment later they were surrounded by four Moroccan policemen who burst out of the palms at a run, their revolvers already drawn. The four constables stopped dead, their feet skidding in the fine sand. Then two of them moved swiftly to support Kerim while the third crouched to inspect the dead body of Zarb. The third man waited warily until a familiar uniformed figure appeared.

Inspector Haffard said calmly,

"I do hope somebody's got some explanations."

★ ★ ★

Back inside the ruined walls of the Foreign Legion blockhouse the crippled Arshid still lay propped on one elbow with his revolver trained on Mohammed who now sprawled face down on the sand with his hands clasped behind his neck. His dusky face grew even darker as he watched two of his colleagues returning through the gateway carrying a body between them, and then he smiled

341

quickly as he recognised Kerim, Alan and Cathy being escorted by Haffard and the remaining two men.

Haffard had extracted most of his explanations at the oasis where Kerim had done most of the talking. Alan had been answering questions on the walk back and now he felt confident enough to ask some of his own.

Haffard grinned at the first one.

"Simple, Mr. Ross, we arrived here so promptly because Sergeant Arshid called us up on the transmitter that we hid so carefully in his Land Rover We have been waiting some six miles away on the camel track ever since we followed you out of Zagora this morning."

Alan stared now at Arshid, who having been relieved of his guard duty was suffering stolidly while one of the constables attended to the bullet wound in his thigh. Arshid smiled broadly.

"I made the call while everybody was watching the three camel riders approach and I was thought to be skulking in the Land Rover in hiding. I had to keep my voice very soft but the radio is powerful.

It is hidden beneath my seat."

Alan felt foolish as he said, "It's still hard to believe that you're a police sergeant. You should have been an actor."

Arshid grinned, "I was, before I became a policeman. I think that is why the Inspector chose me for this job. But I must admit that this part was difficult. To listen to a man sentence you to death and still maintain the pretence that you cannot understand what is being said is beyond anything I have done before. It was difficult too when I walked unsuspecting through the gateway and first confronted you with Zarb. The Egyptian Colonel almost died then, for my hand was already on the gun beneath my djellabah. But you saved his life by attacking him, and Miss Dawson was so swift in picking up his gun that it was safe for me to continue acting. Of course when the camel riders converged on the blockhouse it was obviously time to call up the Inspector, but I admit that I was cursing myself for leaving it too late until the sound of the jeep distracted everybody's attention and allowed me to produce my revolver."

Cathy still stood close by Alan and her expression was slightly baffled. She said slowly,

"But how did you know that we would be coming to you to hire a car?"

"Because — " Arshid winced suddenly as the doctoring constable cleaned his leg. His face tightened and then reverted to its smile with difficulty. "Because the boy at your hotel was paid to bring you to me. The real blacksmith who owns that battered old wreck was also paid to stay out of the way while I took his place."

"But how did you know we would come to Zagora?" Cathy demanded in exasperation.

Haffard answered her. "I think perhaps we should grant Sergeant Arshid a moment's peace until his leg is bandaged. I will tell you everything if you will just have patience and listen."

They faced the Inspector who eyed them severely.

"We have been keeping you young people under observation ever since the guide Achmed and the Rif Sheikh Abd-el-Zeba were murdered in Fez. The day after those murders occurred an unsigned letter arrived in my office in Marrakech. The writer of that letter identified you, Miss Dawson, and you, Mr. Ross, as the mysterious English couple who had been reported at the scene of each crime, and whom the Fez police wished to interview. However, the writer also stressed that you were not responsible, and gave the names and descriptions of the true murderers, namely Colonel Zarb and his two lieutenants. The letter also informed me that Zarb had also arranged the murder of George Dawson, but unfortunately by then I had already released the snake-charmer who had played the leading part in his death.

"However, from there the letter became completely vague. It hinted that our search for Zarb and his two men should be concentrated to the south, and mentioned that you young people would most probably be heading back to Marrakech, but that was all. Quite frankly I considered it the work of a crank, but when the Fez police found your Zephyr car near Ifrane I began to think again. I had my men keep their eyes open in Marrakech and promptly found that Miss Dawson was running round asking questions in the medina."

Cathy looked disappointed. "I didn't think I was that obvious."

Haffard smiled. "Perhaps you would not have been in any other part of the world. But a stranger whose questions do not fit the tourist pattern is quickly marked in the medina. I was tempted to pull you in for questioning then, but an instinct made me give you your heads for a while. You were not running or you would have headed for the coast, and I wanted to find out what it was for which you were searching. A police agent travelled with you on the bus to Ouarzazate, and then a replacement followed you to Zagora. It was obvious that if you wished to go any farther you would attempt to hire a car, so Sergeant Arshid was rushed into position and the hotel clerk given instructions on where to send you. Two men fitting the descriptions given in my mysterious letter were also reported in Zagora and so I came south myself, sensing that things were boiling nicely to a head. Everybody concerned seemed to be gathering in the area. Consequently I followed the Land Rover with my men when the Sergeant drove you into the desert."

Arshid glanced up, his leg now neatly bandaged, and added, "I was able to make a report while you were first exploring the blockhouse. I warned the Inspector to simply wait on the camel track until something definite developed."

Alan looked self-consciously from Arshid to Haffard.

"I suppose we ought to apologise for making things more awkward for you."

Haffard's face became grimly severe. "You were very foolish, both of you. You should have come straight to me with your suspicions about George Dawson's death. I think that if I tried hard enough I could still make out a very solid criminal case of obstructing the course of justice against the pair of you." He glared at them for a long moment, and then a faint trace of amusement glimmered almost unnoticeably in his eyes. He went on. "But perhaps on the other hand if you had not led us here to this ruin in the desert then we should still have a trio of Egyptian killers running loose in my territory. So perhaps I will not press any charges."

Cathy said thankfully, "I'm so glad everything is cleared up."

"Not quite," Haffard reproved. "There is still one outstanding question to be answered." He turned and fixed demanding eyes upon Kerim.

The French-Egyptian had submitted to the amateur doctoring of the constable who had tended Arshid's leg, and now his shirt had been cut away from his shoulder and chest and the last bandages were being fixed. He was still in pain but he managed to smile under Haffard's gaze.

"Your suspicions are correct, Inspector. I did send that unsigned letter. It was very carefully prepared for it had conflicting motives. First I hoped that you would detain Miss Dawson and Mr. Ross, it seemed the only way of keeping them out of my way and protecting their lives from Zarb after I had found that they could not be scared off. Second I wished to present you with enough evidence to track down Zarb if I failed, but not enough to enable you to reach him before I had made my own personal attempt to settle the score."

Kerim moved closer, drawing the cloak of his white burnous over his bandaged shoulder.

"You see, Inspector, Zarb was not working as a private individual. The Cairo Government has been sending arms south to the rebel elements in the Congo for a long time now, and is finding the project somewhat expensive. The presence of the fortune from the lost caravan here in south Morocco would have provided them with an easy answer. The caravan could have been reformed and sent south across the desert with much less risk than would have been involved in smuggling the spoils north.

The proceeds would have paid for more rebel arms and helped the Egyptians to maintain their promises without draining the Cairo funds."

Kerim smiled and finished. "I knew that it was quite possible that Zarb would kill me instead of me killing him. And in that event I had to be sure that you would be close enough behind me to take over and ensure that the money for more arms never reached an already bloody battlefield."

Haffard nodded. "So now everything is explained — but where is this lost fortune from the past? Where is it buried?"

Kerim's face darkened regretfully. "I don't know. As a son I did not know my father very well, or he might have shared his secret with me. I had not seen him for several years before the night Zarb took me from my cell to the café and he attempted to barter for my life. The story he told was as new to me as it was to Zarb. But — " He turned to gesture to the body that the two constables had covered with their jackets in the shadow of the wall. "Zarb took the notes my father offered him. No doubt he still has them."

Haffard hesitated, and then nodded. Kerim walked slowly towards the Egyptian's body and the Inspector went with him. They searched carefully, and after a few moments they returned. Haffard held a small and very grubby notebook that had a look of eternal age. He stopped with Kerim beside him and then handed it back to the French-Egyptian.

"You read it. Perhaps you are more accustomed to your father's writing."

Kerim nodded. He read slowly.

"There is a cluster of bright red rocks in the desert, four large rocks the size of mules, and seven smaller ones the height of a man's knee. There is a deep crack between the two biggest rocks. From the rocks to the blockhouse one walks in a straight line, with the setting sun always exactly behind him, balanced on the rim of the desert. The distance is seven thousand, four hundred and thirty six regulation Legion marching paces with full pack."

Kerim looked up and said quietly, "A legionaire's life consisted of marching. Counting the marching paces must have been my father's only way of measuring distance."

Haffard turned to where the lowering sun formed a background of fire behind the west wall of the outpost, throwing a now massive, fortified shadow of black across the golden sand. The rest of them turned with him and Alan and Cathy squinted their eyes against the red glory that rippled across the sky above the ramparts.

Haffard said, equally quietly, "So all we have to do is to walk out there into the sunset. It won't be easy to find after all these years, but the rock pile won't have moved and with a systematic search it will only need time."

Kerim nodded. "Zarb would undoubtedly have invented some good excuse to search the area, a supposed archaeological expedition of some sort to cover his real motives." He looked at Haffard and finished. "But that fortune belonged to the Rif tribes, and now that they are part of the united kingdom of Morocco then it should be returned to the Moroccan government.

There was a moment of solemn quiet as Haffard accepted the dead legionaire's notes, and the sun dipped silently beyond the walls, leaving only the dying red blaze of it passing.

20

An Hotel in Casablanca

Four weeks later Alan Ross stood just inside the doorway of a luxurious hotel suite and made repeated, self-conscious attempts to hurry the departure of a bubbling manager who insisted on detailing every single one of the apartment's seemingly unlimited attractions. The man finally accepted the hint with the startled look of one who has just made a great discovery and spent the next five minutes in profusely apologising as he backed away. Alan closed the door behind him and turned to Cathy who wore a smart blue costume, a tiny hat made up of imitation white and blue petals and a huge unembarrassed smile as she stood in the centre of their pile of suitcases. Her smile was infectious and he grinned in turn as he moved towards her.

"Wasn't it marvellous," she said

dreamily. "All expenses paid by air back to Morocco, a car to whisk us away from the airfield. And now this — the best and biggest suite in the best and biggest hotel in Casablanca."

"It's only just starting to get wonderful," he said firmly. He pulled her into his arms and allowed the sweet taste of her lips to ease the burning desire that had built up inside him. Then there was a smart knock on the door.

"Damn," he said. He kissed her hard, squeezed even harder, and then reluctantly went to open the door.

Haffard stood there, resplendent in his best uniform, the gold braid gleaming on his shoulder bars. He touched his peaked cap and smiled.

"May I offer my congratulations?"

Alan made an effort to sound sincere.

"Of course, Inspector, please come in. After all, we do have you to thank for all this."

Haffard removed his cap and tucked it beneath his arm as he stepped inside the room. He glanced appreciatively around the lush fittings and then smiled again.

"It was not all my doing. The Moroccan government proved very grateful when it recovered the spoils from the lost caravan. It took almost three weeks to find that cleft in the rocks where the fortune had been buried, but it was well worth the effort. The silks had mostly rotted, but the gold, jewels and ivory, which must have constituted a mighty fortune forty years ago have increased greatly by present day standards. Morocco can afford to be generous."

Cathy smiled and then looked serious. "How is Sergeant Arshid?" she asked.

Haffard turned in her direction. "I was coming to that. The Sergeant's leg is healing well and he is able to walk again with a stick. Soon he will be able to throw the stick away and return to duty — as an Inspector this time, his recommendation for promotion has already been approved. He also wishes me to add his congratulations to my own."

Cathy smiled and her cheeks flushed faintly.

Haffard went on, "Your friend Kerim is also back among the ranks of the fit.

He is still wanted for his spying activities by the Egyptian Government, and so he has quietly left for the United States. No doubt the Americans will send him back into North Africa when memories have had time to become blurred, for I gained the impression that he was very valuable to them.

"There is one last item which may interest you, although it is less pleasant. The man you knew as Mohammed has confessed to the murder of Sheikh Abd-el-Zeba and has been sentenced to death. It was of course his comrade who killed the guide Achmed. They knew that Achmed had friends in the dye market who would hide him in trouble and so it was easy to intercept him."

Haffard drew himself to attention and finished.

"And now I must return to my duties. Do not fail to enjoy yourselves in Casablanca."

His eyes were twinkling and Cathy reddened a little before she could smile and thank him. Alan saw him out of the suite and then carefully and deliberately locked the door. He turned round and held the key aloft.

"It was very nice of him to call," he admitted. "But I think we can manage without any further interruptions. After all, this is supposed to be a honeymoon."

And his bride touched the golden band on her finger and smilingly agreed.

THE END

A FOOT IN THE GRAVE
Bruce Marshall

About to be imprisoned and tortured in Buenos Aires, John Smith escapes, only to become involved in an aeroplane hijacking.

DEAD TROUBLE
Martin Carroll

Trespassing brought Jennifer Denning more than she bargained for. She was totally unprepared for the violence which was to lie in her path.

HOURS TO KILL
Ursula Curtiss

Margaret went to New Mexico to look after her sick sister's rented house and felt a sharp edge of fear when the absent landlady arrived.

THE DEATH OF ABBE DIDIER
Richard Grayson

Inspector Gautier of the Sûreté investigates three crimes which are strangely connected.

NIGHTMARE TIME
Hugh Pentecost

Have the missing major and his wife met with foul play somewhere in the Beaumont Hotel, or is their disappearance a carefully planned step in an act of treason?

BLOOD WILL OUT
Margaret Carr

Why was the manor house so oddly familiar to Elinor Howard? Who would have guessed that a Sunday School outing could lead to murder?

THE DRACULA MURDERS
Philip Daniels

The Horror Ball was interrupted by a spectral figure who warned the merrymakers they were tampering with the unknown.

THE LADIES
OF LAMBTON GREEN
Liza Shepherd

Why did murdered Robin Colquhoun's picture pose such a threat to the ladies of Lambton Green?

CARNABY
AND THE GAOLBREAKERS
Peter N. Walker

Detective Sergeant James Aloysius Carnaby-King is sent to prison as bait. When he joins in an escape he is thrown headfirst into a vicious murder hunt.